THE LEGEND OF THE
LOST JEWELS

THE LEGEND OF THE
LOST JEWELS

A HAZEL FRUMP ADVENTURE

JENNIFER LANTHIER

HarperTrophyCanada™

An imprint of HarperCollinsPublishersLtd

The Legend of the Lost Jewels
© 2008 by Jennifer Lanthier. All rights
reserved.

Published by HarperTrophyCanada™, an
imprint of HarperCollins Publishers Ltd

HarperTrophyCanada™ is a trademark
of HarperCollins Publishers.

First edition

HarperCollins books may be purchased
for educational, business, or sales
promotional use through our Special
Markets Department.

HarperCollins Publishers Ltd
2 Bloor Street East, 20th Floor
Toronto, Ontario, Canada
M4W 1A8

www.harpercollins.ca

Library and Archives Canada
Cataloguing in Publication

Lanthier, Jennifer
The legend of the lost jewels / Jennifer
Lanthier. (A Hazel Frump adventure)

ISBN 978-0-00-639161-6

I. Title. II. Series: Lanthier, Jennifer.
Hazel Frump adventure.

PS8623.A699L43 2008   JC813'.6
C2008-900867-7

HC 9 8 7 6 5 4 3 2 1

Printed and bound in the United States

Design by Sharon Kish

For Nicky, Buzz and James

CHAPTER ONE

"**I** don't know where I am."

Her throat so raw that she couldn't make her voice work properly, Hazel Frump whispered into the darkness. The raging wind caught her words and whipped them away, but there was no one to hear them anyway. No one else was crazy enough to be out in this storm.

In all of her twelve years, Hazel had never felt so alone, so cold, so wet, so weary, and so utterly lost. Her clothes were soaked through to her skin and she could no longer feel her toes and fingers. Soon she would have to stop walking. She would lie down right here in the woods, in the freezing October rain, and let the wind howl around her. She guessed that would probably kill her. She was too tired to care.

It had seemed like a good idea at the time. Hazel and her brother, Ned, were supposed to spend their Thanksgiving break with Uncle Seamus and the cousins at Land's End on Île du Loup. When an outbreak of flu sent her boarding school into a tizzy, Hazel had simply decided to head to the castle on Île du Loup a day early.

"You're sure they're expecting you?"

Despite her rheumy eyes, hacking cough and sweat-soaked shirt, Ms. Craven was one of the few staff members not confined to bed. The virus had hit hard and dizzyingly fast, plunging the school into disorder and confusion. Dozens of parents called to insist healthy students be put on the first train home; dozens more began arriving at the northern Ontario school to personally collect their sick children.

Clearly, Ms. Craven would be relieved to be rid of Hazel. So the girl had nodded, fingers crossed behind her back, and joined the group of students boarding the train for eastern Ontario.

In fact, Hazel had tried to call Land's End but there'd been no answer. She hadn't worried—phones at the rambling Victorian castle were prone to breaking down, especially during storms, and a nasty weather system was already sweeping across the province.

By the time the train pulled into Frontenac, on the northeastern shore of Lake Ontario, Hazel had decided she might as well surprise everyone. During the rough ferry crossing to the island, it did occur to her that perhaps she ought to phone the castle again. But that wouldn't have been as much fun. So Hazel had ignored the worsening storm and concentrated instead on imagining Uncle Seamus's shocked delight when he opened the door and found her standing on the steps.

Except the shock was all Hazel's.

The taxi had let her off at the bottom of the long, slippery driveway, and she'd shouldered her pack and trudged up the icy road, picturing the warmth of the castle and the welcome she'd get. Of course, Matt and Mark, the twins, wouldn't be home yet from university. Still, eight-year-old Oliver would be there to gaze at her in admiration, and bossy Deirdre would make her hot chocolate, and fuss and scold.

But when Hazel reached the hilltop, no smoke curled from

any of the chimneys; no light shone from any of the tall, Gothic windows. Rain and sleet had turned the grey stone walls a forbidding black. With its fairy-tale turrets and battlements, Land's End usually seemed to have sprung from the pages of a storybook. Now it was a hostile fortress. Hazel pounded on door after door, but each one was shut tight against the storm and securely locked.

She was alone.

She was stuck outside in rain that was rapidly turning to ice and wind that was almost strong enough to knock her down. And not one person in the whole world knew. Nobody was expecting her until tomorrow night. Her uncle and cousins could be anywhere. They could be in the village, picking up some groceries, or at a café. They could be home in five minutes . . . or five hours. Or they could be out of town.

"Brilliant." Hazel hadn't meant to say the word out loud but it wasn't like there was anyone around to hear. "What is it with holidays?"

Last summer vacation had started with the disappearance and wrongful imprisonment of her father. She'd thought that was bad. But she'd had her brother, Ned, and together they had saved their dad and reunited him with Uncle Seamus and the cousins. If only she'd waited for Ned this time, before coming to the island. But his boarding school didn't have a flu outbreak, and she had been so eager to get to the castle.

Hazel tugged the zipper higher on her thin jacket and pulled off her sopping backpack. The jacket didn't provide much cover from the wind, as she crouched on the floor of the porch in front of the locked kitchen door. She couldn't stay here. She had to come up with a plan. Now.

"I could hike back to the village," Hazel told the stone gargoyle squatting in a corner of the porch, "or I could break a window and get into the castle that way . . ." She gazed at the limestone walls that stretched toward the sky. The few windows within her reach were works of art. Their stained glass had withstood storms, vandals, errant hockey pucks and fly balls for more than a hundred and fifty years. They were irreplaceable—she couldn't bear to smash one.

Hazel sighed. If only there was another way in . . .

"Oh! The tunnels—I'll just go to the cave and get in that way!"

The idea was so simple and perfect that it sent warmth tingling through her tired limbs. An old smugglers' tunnel in the castle's cellar led to a cave at a nearby beach. The hike from here to the cave would be nasty—it might be nearly as far to the village, although in the opposite direction. But once inside the cave, she'd be out of the rain and wind and could make her way back through the tunnel to the castle cellar.

Taking a piece of paper and a pencil from her backpack, she scribbled a note to her cousins explaining where she had gone, just in case they returned to the castle before she did. Hazel wedged the paper under a corner of the gargoyle. Then she headed out again into the storm.

The cave was not at the first beach Hazel came to, but at a second, farther cove. Finding it should have been a simple task; she just had to keep the shore of Lake Ontario to her right, and the woods to her left. But the way was hard going. The wind shrieked and moaned and seemed to gather strength with every step she took. The rain felt more and more like tiny daggers of ice cutting into her skin.

The weather forced Hazel deeper into the woods, seeking shelter. That made it difficult to keep her bearings. Sometimes she thought she was following a trail, but moments later the path would disappear, and the trees and shrubs would close around her. Frozen brambles pulled at her hair and wet leaves slapped her face. Hazel's throat began to ache and her head hurt. Her legs, at first tired and sore, gradually grew numb. From time to time Hazel stumbled, and twice she fell on the icy ground. Once she stepped in a puddle that went all the way up to her knees, and from then on she couldn't feel her toes.

"C'mon, you're a Frump, aren't you?" Hazel whispered. She'd said the same thing to her cousin Oliver last summer, urging him to stand up to a local bully. But the words seemed hollow now. What did it mean to be a Frump, anyway? To be good at keeping secrets and getting into danger?

Time had turned as slippery as the ground beneath her feet. The rain was turning into snow. Hazel was certain she had been walking for hours, maybe even all night. She must have passed the beach already. Was she going in circles? She was never going to find the cave, never going to reach the tunnel. She might as well lie down and rest. The next time she fell, Hazel wouldn't have the strength to get up again, she just knew it. Maybe she was already asleep—this didn't feel real anymore. It felt like a dream. A horrible dream.

Someone tapped her on the shoulder. Hazel jumped. Her heart beating wildly, she spun around. But the forest was empty.

She took a deep breath and rubbed her eyes with a sodden glove. She must have been dozing. There was no one. Except for a hawk, perched on a frozen branch so close she could almost have stretched out her finger and touched him. His head was turned sideways and he was staring at Hazel with one golden eye. Hazel had never been this close to a wild bird! Surely now that he'd seen her he'd fly away? Hazel waited. So did the hawk. It was almost as if he wanted her to do something. But what?

No. She was hallucinating; it was the fatigue and the cold. She needed to lie down. Hazel closed her eyes and felt her body sway.

Another tap on her shoulder.

Opening her eyes, Hazel found herself staring into a hollow in the trunk of the tree just below the hawk's perch. The woods were pitch black all around her, but somehow the storm clouds must have parted just long enough for a ray of light from the moon or the stars to pierce the canopy of leaves. Something had glinted from inside the tree. Hazel reached into the hollow. Her numb fingers scrabbled uselessly for a few moments before closing around something small and hard. When she drew out her hand, it was clenching a frozen bit of metal.

The hawk tilted its head and gave a cry of triumph. As Hazel watched, he rose into the air, but settled on a tree only a short distance away. There was something not quite right about the way he flew, as if he were being pulled off balance. Was he injured?

Hazel shoved the piece of metal into her pocket. She took a step toward the bird, and then another. He watched her, waiting. But when she was almost close enough to touch him, the hawk soared into the air again. And again, he alighted on a nearby branch—and waited.

It was like a game. Hazel's body still ached and she was so dizzy she felt her head might tumble off her shoulders. But she followed the hawk. He moved again and again, waiting each time for Hazel to catch up. Sometimes he flew so far that all Hazel could see was a faint blur on a distant stump. But he always waited until she drew close enough to touch him before taking off again.

Presently, Hazel became aware of a new sound. Not the scratching of the icy rain or the howling of the wind—a duller, more insistent sound, like a soft roar. There was something familiar about it. The hawk circled high above the treetops, then swooped low. Hazel couldn't see where the bird went but she could follow its piercing shriek. As she stumbled forward, the roaring grew louder.

All of a sudden, the woods fell away behind her and Hazel was standing on a rise overlooking the shore of Lake Ontario, her ears filled with the sound of waves pounding the beach. There, a few feet away, was the entrance to the tunnel.

Forgetting all about the bird and how exhausted she was, Hazel broke into a run. Clambering over the icy rocks at the cave's entrance, she fell again. But she didn't care. Once inside the cave, it was as if someone had flipped a switch, shutting off the storm. Walls of earth and stone several feet thick blotted out all sound of the wind and rain. The air was still cold enough to sting her cheeks, but at least the cave was dry and quiet. The first time she had been in it, the darkness of the tunnel had scared her a little, but now Hazel was so determined to get to the castle, she had no time for fear. She stumbled down the passageway, tears of relief pricking her eyes. The journey was long and painful, but she didn't stop until she reached the door to the castle cellar.

It was locked.

A sob of protest escaped her. The cousins had always bragged that they never locked their doors. What was going on? Hazel closed her eyes. Her head felt strange—sort of light and fuzzy. The floor of the passageway tilted suddenly and she slid to the ground.

CHAPTER TWO

"The doctor's best guess is that you were exposed to the virus at your school. Then you wore yourself out with that trek through the storm. Your body simply couldn't cope."

Uncle Seamus smiled at Hazel. It took some effort for her to smile back. She'd felt great waking up and finding herself safe and warm, tucked in her bed in the tower room. But she wasn't at all happy to learn she'd still be stuck here for a week after the Thanksgiving break, recuperating. Hazel *liked* her boarding school. And her basketball team had important games coming up. Georgia Chandler would have to take her place as point guard. She was younger than Hazel but she was good. Too good.

"Look on the bright side—you should have your voice back by tomorrow." Uncle Seamus patted her shoulder. "And with proper rest and nutrition, you'll be up and about in a day or two. You'll just need to take it easy, as the doctor said. Land's End is a big place—you'll get enough exercise just making your way from your bedroom to the kitchen!" He was right, of course. The castle was so large it would have made a great hotel, and it was crammed full of interesting things, like suits of armour and old tapestries. Hazel knew there were plenty of rooms and passageways she had yet to explore.

As Uncle Seamus headed to his study to telephone Hazel's father and her school, he held the door open for her brother, Ned, and three of their cousins: Oliver, Deirdre and Matt. None of them resembled Hazel in the least. Of course, that made sense when it came to seventeen-year-old Matt and his non-identical twin, Mark. Adopted at the age of six, after the death of their Trinidadian mother, neither teen could possibly have shared Hazel's green, almond-shaped eyes, pale skin or unruly mane of flame-coloured hair.

But Hazel looked nothing like her biological relatives, either. At fourteen, Deirdre was roughly Hazel's height, but she wore her sandy hair short, and her soft brown eyes were as round as buttons. As for Ned and Oliver, they could almost have been twins, sharing the same dark, ruler-straight hair, slight build and wire-rimmed glasses. Not to mention a worry that their growth spurts might never come.

Just now, all of the Frumps wore a look of deep concern, and Hazel could tell it was for her.

She struggled to sit upright as the solemn procession filed into the room. She had lots of questions, but apparently she also had laryngitis. That figured. Hazel picked up the pen and pad of paper Uncle Seamus had left her and wrote:

So who locked the tunnel door?

Matt gave her a sympathetic look. "Actually, that door wasn't locked."

Hazel's eyes widened in disbelief. But Matt continued, "As soon as we got home and found your note, I ran downstairs. You were passed out on the tunnel side of the door. It wasn't locked, but Dad figures you were so tired and confused you couldn't get it open. You must have pushed when you should have pulled."

Hazel didn't know whether to cry or laugh. The door wasn't locked? Matt had to be joking. But Deirdre was nodding her head violently.

"What I can't understand is why you didn't just let yourself into the kitchen, you goose!" Frustration was written all over Deirdre's face. "You could have died of exposure or something."

As Matt shot his sister a warning look, Hazel picked up the pencil and wrote, slowly this time:

What do you mean?

"You know: the spare key that we leave under the stone gargoyle!" Deirdre was frowning now. "You had to have seen it—you left your note right beside it! Why didn't you just use it to let yourself in?"

Hazel swallowed hard. There were gaps in her memory, perhaps caused by the virus. She remembered arriving at the castle and finding it locked. Yet about the journey through the woods she recalled almost nothing—it was a blur, like a dream—and all she could see were images of snow and slush and rain. But she would never forget the moment she reached the cellar door.

And none of that would have happened, if only she had noticed the key.

A hand gripped Hazel's shoulder awkwardly. She looked up into the round spectacles of her ten-year-old brother. Ned was a certified genius; there was no way *he* would have missed a spare key. But he loved her. Hazel knew he'd say something to cheer her up.

"You were already pretty sick by the time you got to the castle," Ned said. "I overheard the doctor telling Uncle Seamus you would've been too sick to think straight."

Hazel nodded, and managed a little smile.

"Of course you *never* think straight," Ned continued, "but I didn't tell *them* that."

Hazel's smile wobbled.

"The doctor said it's a miracle you're okay. But Uncle Seamus said it was because you're really strong and a great athlete . . . and one of the most pigheaded people he's ever met." Ned's expression was thoughtful. "He said you were like a mule, if a mule was more stubborn."

That was enough cheering up. Hazel grabbed the paper again and wrote:

Where's Mark?

"Over at Charlotte's, giving her a hand with some damage from the storm," Matt said. "They should be here soon."

Good. Charlotte was pretty laid-back, for an adult. A distant cousin, in her twenties, she wore a wide grin and a year-round tan from spending so much time out of doors. She lived just a few miles away, and when Uncle Seamus had to travel he often left her in charge. This made all the Frumps happy because Charlotte was a good deal less strict than most adults.

But Hazel was most looking forward to seeing Mark. When he entered a room everyone perked up. It was as if someone had switched on the radio. Mark was strikingly different from his twin. The shorter, solid Matt often seemed older than his years, with a buttoned-down personality to match his golf shirts and close-shaved hair. Mark was a lean, lanky goof, constantly experimenting with his appearance. Deirdre said he started trends just for the fun of breaking them.

Hazel wondered whether university would help Mark solve his dilemma of whether to be a lawyer, like Uncle Seamus, or a great chef.

"They'd better be quick." Deirdre's voice was stern. "We're counting on Mark to get back in time to put the finishing touches on Thanksgiving dinner. He's the best cook in this house."

Hazel stared. Thanksgiving? But that wasn't until Monday. She'd arrived on Thursday—the tenth of October. Just how much time had passed while she'd been ill?

"It's Sunday morning," Matt said, reading her alarmed expression. "We're celebrating Thanksgiving early because of your dad. Uncle Colin was able to wrangle a couple of days off from whatever top-secret thing he's helping Interpol with now. He's flying in from Paris later today. That is, if the storm doesn't hold him up."

Hazel looked at Ned and saw her own joy reflected there. They hadn't expected to see their father until Christmas! The cousins quickly filled Hazel in on what else she'd missed. The storm had wreaked havoc on highways, and had brought down trees and power lines all across eastern Canada. Uncle Seamus and Mark had been driving back from McGill University in Montreal when it hit. The icy roads had forced them to a crawl and eventually they had checked into a motel rather than continue driving. And at the time Hazel was pounding on the castle door, Deirdre and Oliver were in Frontenac, having dinner at the university with Matt.

"We almost stayed at Matt's dorm in town because of the freezing rain," Oliver said in a small voice, as if confessing a crime. "If we had, you would have been stuck in that tunnel overnight."

"Well, it's a good thing we didn't." Deirdre's voice was brisk. "Anyway, we were never really going to stay in Frontenac overnight, Oliver. We both had too much homework waiting for us."

Matt gave Hazel a sober look. "I wasn't sure we'd made the right call, when I saw how bad the roads were on the island. But when we found your note, we knew . . ."

". . . that we'd done the right thing," Deirdre said, a note of triumph in her voice.

". . . that we'd gotten lucky," Matt corrected her. "We got home around ten, and I ran straight to the cellar and found you. But when you wrote your note, you said it was just after six o'clock. Dad said the doctor figures you spent most of that time outside."

Hazel shivered. Before anyone else could speak, the door burst open. In strode Mark. His jeans were slathered in mud and his lumberjack shirt reeked of sweat. The neat cornrows he'd worn all summer were gone, replaced by a loose 'fro. Hazel had seen the lanky teen less than two months ago, but she was sure Mark already looked taller.

"Little cousin! You're looking a lot better than the last time I saw you." Mark made as if to flop down beside her, but Deirdre blocked his way.

"Stop. You're sopping wet and —oh, you stink! What have you and Charlotte been up to?"

Mark patted his sister annoyingly on the head and flashed a grin at Hazel. "It's called Being a Good Neighbour, sis. A whole lot of trees are down across lanes and driveways, and, unlike Dad, Charlotte lets me use the power saw. And she wanted to check on Kenny Pritchard and his mum, too. Considering how Kenny used to bully Oliver, being neighbourly to him wasn't my idea of a priority. But you know how soft-hearted Charlotte is. With Mr. Pritchard in jail, Mrs. Pritchard's been having a tough time managing the farm on her own."

Hazel's eyes met Ned's. They were responsible for Kenny's dad being in jail. He was part of a gang of thieves and smugglers that she and Ned had captured in the summer, using Ned's special stink bombs to trap them at a Martello tower until the police arrived. The leader of the gang was Kenny's uncle Clive Pritchard, an art forger and con man. The Pritchard brothers were in jail now, awaiting trial. In Hazel's mind that had been the end of the adventure. She'd never considered what happened afterward, to people like Kenny and his mother. Until now.

Matt gestured toward Hazel's window. "It's a mess out there. That cold snap seems to be disappearing just as fast as it came and now all the ice is melting so quickly, they're worried about flooding."

"Happy Thanksgiving, everyone." Deirdre shook her head. "Speaking of which, Mark, what about our turkey?"

"And the pies," Oliver added.

"O ye of little—no, make that zero—faith. The turkey's been in the oven since before I headed to Charly's this morning. And I baked the mincemeat pies yesterday." Mark's tone was aggrieved. "Do I take it the five of you have just been sitting around, waiting for me to come back and prepare the feast?"

Before anyone could answer, Uncle Seamus reappeared.

"Everybody out! My niece needs her rest. And each of you has work to do, if we're going to have a proper Thanksgiving. It can't be all up to Mark. The rest of you go, go—oh, go peel potatoes!"

"I *always* have to peel potatoes," Deirdre muttered under her breath. But she steered Oliver to the door with one hand, while motioning to her other brothers to follow.

Ned lingered by Hazel's bed.

"When Uncle Seamus met me at the train station last night he said you were sleeping. He said I shouldn't worry, because your fever had broken. It didn't sound too serious. But . . . Hazel, you don't look so good."

Hazel squeezed her brother's arm. She wrote as quickly as she could:

I'll be fine—can't wait to see Dad!

Ned squeezed back. He and Hazel had worked hard during the summer to reunite their father with the rest of his family, but it wasn't like snapping your fingers. Back at boarding school, the first letter Hazel had received from her father contained an excellent excuse for missing Thanksgiving—Interpol had asked him to help solve another art theft. Hazel had been disappointed, but hardly surprised. Though patience wasn't one of her virtues, she knew it would take time for Colin Frump to feel comfortable back at Land's End.

Knowing their father had changed his plans and would be here for Thanksgiving gave Hazel a warm and cozy feeling. As Ned slipped out of the room, she snuggled deeper under her covers. It was impossible to keep her eyes open a moment longer.

She was back in the woods, and she could see a light flickering up ahead—a warm, dancing light that made her think of fire. Hazel paused. Was it safe? Who would make a fire in these woods? But the hawk was beckoning her to follow. As she pushed her way through a dense thicket, Hazel stumbled and fell. Strange—instead of landing on frozen earth and snow, she found herself on a Persian carpet. And just a few feet away a fire was blazing merrily on a stone hearth. Hazel rubbed her eyes. She wasn't in the woods anymore; she was in the library at Land's End. For a moment she felt relief, but then something else—a prickling sensation that told her she wasn't alone. Somewhere nearby, she heard a girl crying. When the girl spoke, the fear and misery in her voice struck a chill in Hazel's heart: "What has he done? What has he done?"

Hazel's eyes flew open. Sweat was trickling down her temples and she was tangled in blankets. Sunlight streamed through the Gothic windows of her tower room. As her heartbeat returned to normal, she wondered what the dream meant. It had seemed so real, more real than any dream she'd had before. Except one. For years, Hazel had been plagued by a recurring dream about being trapped in a tower. That dream had finally stopped after she and Ned solved the mystery of their mother's death.

Hazel shook her head slightly, trying to clear it. This was different, she told herself. It was just a dream—a random, meaningless dream. There was no mystery to solve.

was some time before Hazel could relax enough to let
m her again.

. . . .

Colin Frump hadn't arrived by the time Matt and Uncle
Seamus escorted Hazel down to dinner, but Charlotte had,
and she wrapped her arms around Hazel in an enormous hug.
The sight of the long table in the formal dining hall groaning
beneath the weight of all the food took everyone's breath
away. Hazel's mouth watered at the array of silver platters
and bowls loaded with turkey, gravy, two kinds of dressing,
cranberry sauce, wild rice, salads, mincemeat pie, roasted yams,
mashed turnip and potatoes. Lots of potatoes. They'd been
mashed, roasted, baked and scalloped—no wonder Deirdre
hated peeling.

Mark was in his element. He described each dish in detail
before anyone was allowed to begin, obviously taking special
pride in his pies.

"I give you apple, rhubarb, peach and mixed-berry pies. And
my homage to the province of Quebec, a sugar pie."

That Thanksgiving dinner was the best Hazel and Ned had
ever had. Neither of them had heard of sugar pie, but Mark said
it was the greatest thing he'd discovered at McGill University,
so they made sure to save room. It wasn't easy. Everything
tasted delicious—even, to Hazel's amazement, the turnip.
Dinner lasted so long that Hazel had to take a break, stretching out on a sofa in the corner of the room, that had been made
up with sheets and pillows for her. From there, she listened to
the hum of voices. Contentment spread from her full belly to
the tips of her toes. Only one thing was keeping this night from
perfection—

"Did I miss dinner?" Colin Frump asked from the doorway.

Hazel's laryngitis wouldn't let her speak, but she found the strength to move faster than she could have imagined. She got there before anyone else, flinging her arms around her father, even as Uncle Seamus was just pushing back his chair. She had to let go almost as quickly—hugging him was like hugging a melting icicle.

"Dad!" Ned had joined her at their father's side. "Yikes. You're as cold as a Popsicle and a whole lot wetter!"

"Yes, I'm afraid I am." Colin sent an apologetic look in his brother's direction. "It's raining again. I'm afraid there's been some flooding. I had to abandon my car at the bridge near the village and walk. I let myself in, but I didn't stop to change in case the food was running out. You haven't eaten it all, have you? I heard there was going to be pie."

His wistful tone brought Deirdre to his side.

"Uncle Colin, there's *tons* of food and we haven't even touched the pies yet. But Ned's right, you're sopping wet. Go get into dry clothes and we'll reheat some of these dishes."

Twenty minutes later, they were all back at the table, Hazel and Ned sitting on either side of their father. Deirdre's eyes opened wide as Mark gleefully handed Colin Frump a plate with three slices of pie.

"Here, Uncle, why not start with dessert and work your way backward to the turkey."

"Right," Colin agreed after a moment's pause. "And this way you can all join me, instead of waiting until I finish."

Mark grinned. "Exactly."

As they all helped themselves to generous servings of pie, Hazel glanced at the lines etched across her father's forehead and wondered what he was thinking about. He suddenly seemed much older than Uncle Seamus. That was amazing because they were identical twins, and people usually relied on Uncle Seamus's beard to tell them apart. Her father met her eyes and gave her a tired smile.

"It looks like I'll be out of the country for a while, with this Interpol thing, but when I heard about Hazel's ill-timed notion to take up wilderness hiking, I just had to come."

Her velvet-covered chair was soft and comfy, but Hazel suddenly felt like squirming. At least with laryngitis she couldn't be expected to answer.

Her father shifted his gaze from her worried face to Uncle Seamus's resigned one. The brothers exchanged rueful smiles.

Colin Frump shrugged. "Oh well, Seamus and I made our share of questionable decisions when we were your age. And I suppose you put yourself through a far worse punishment than anything I could dream up."

Uncle Seamus fixed Hazel with a stern look. "Nonetheless, young lady, the next time you decide to surprise us . . . *don't*."

Hazel nodded. Across the table, Charlotte rolled her eyes.

"Now, I have some news for you and Ned," their father announced. "The storm wreaked havoc across the northern part of the province. The heads of your schools have been in touch, and the damage to those buildings has been severe. Both schools will be closed until the first week of November. If it's all right with your uncle, you'll have to stay here."

Ned began polishing his spectacles furiously. "This is terrible—I'm in the middle of a crucial experiment at school. What about the emergency generators? Does the lab still have power? If the temperature fluctuates too much, I'm a goner."

Oliver made a sympathetic face, but Mark laughed. "Ned, you're missing the big picture here: *no school!*"

Deirdre sighed. "This is so wasted on you guys. You *like* school. Why couldn't it be me? I'd give anything to skip English class for a few weeks."

Hazel thought about all the catching up she'd have to do when school reopened. Her teachers would go nuts, piling on work. On the other hand, no school for anyone meant no losing her spot to Georgia Chandler. And it might be fun to spend Halloween at the castle. She wondered if Deirdre still dressed up and went trick-or-treating.

"Ned, your science and math teachers have assigned some extra work for most of the students, but not for you. The head says you work too hard in those areas as it is. She suggested you use this time to take a break, perhaps focus on other interests." Colin Frump looked quizzically at his son. "Do you *have* other interests?"

Mark snorted. Ned shot him a look.

"Hey, remember those experiments with toxic mould you were working on at the end of the summer?" Oliver's voice rose in excitement. "We could start those up again!"

Colin Frump's eyes narrowed. "Perhaps Ned's school has a point." Turning to Hazel, he said, "This mystery virus you're recovering from has struck many of your fellow students as well, so there's only one assignment coming your way. The history teacher will e-mail the details, but I gather you're to write an essay about what life would have been like for your ancestors in the nineteenth century."

"Lucky you're here," Matt said. "You can probably find everything you need right in the Land's End library."

Hazel had been happily mulling the prospect of hanging out at Land's End with Ned, but Matt's words jolted her back to her dream. She could see the fire burning in the library hearth, and hear the girl crying, *"What has he done?"* She shivered.

"Hey, do you guys know the legend of the lost jewels?" Deirdre asked. "Maybe you could put in some stuff about that."

Colin Frump stroked his chin. "Now that's something I haven't heard since I was a boy. The legend of the lost jewels . . . Remember all the hours we spent searching for them, Seamus?"

Uncle Seamus smiled. "All my kids have looked too. They took the entire castle apart, trying to find them. But to no avail. I suspect it was nothing more than a family myth."

Hazel and Ned exchanged glances. Wasn't anyone going to explain? As if reading their minds, Matt leaned forward.

"Nobody really knows the details, but the story's been handed down through the years. Supposedly, some ancestor or other lost a bunch of jewels somewhere in the castle and they were never found. I used to think it was just a story Dad invented to get us to tidy up around the place. You know: 'Clean out your closet—the lost jewels could be hiding at the bottom.'"

"Maybe you'll find out more about the jewels while you're researching." Deirdre set her fork down. "Any kind of information would be good. We don't even know what jewels were lost . . . I always pictured ropes of pearls and gold bracelets."

Colin Frump had a gleam in his eye.

"I've just had an idea . . . a way for Hazel and Ned to fend off boredom while they're here. But I may need some help."

Charlotte nodded. "I'd be delighted."

"I'm afraid I'll be putting in long hours in Frontenac, in court and at the office." Uncle Seamus sighed. "Life certainly could be dull for Hazel and Ned once their cousins return to school."

"Yeah, one thing we know for sure about Hazel and Ned— left to their own devices, they won't get up to anything." Mark shook his head. "They couldn't find an adventure if they tripped over it!"

Ned looked at Hazel, one eyebrow raised.

"Doesn't anyone here know the meaning of the word *jinx*?"

"You mean, when two people say the same thing at the same time?" Oliver looked puzzled.

Charlotte grinned. "I think he's talking about a hex or a curse—you think we're asking for trouble, don't you, Ned?"

"That's crazy talk," Matt said. He pushed back his chair and began clearing plates.

Uncle Seamus and Colin Frump nodded and then said, at exactly the same time:

"What could possibly go wrong?"

There was a moment's pause before the entire room erupted into laughter—except for Hazel, who couldn't make a sound, and Ned, who wore a dour expression.

"Jinx," Ned said bitterly.

CHAPTER THREE

It took more than a week for the jinx to catch up with Hazel and Ned. And when it did, it came without warning, like a sudden push into an icy pool. Because until that moment, Hazel and Ned were exquisitely happy. At least a dozen times each day, they exchanged glances that said, *Can you believe how lucky we are?* None of their classmates was spending the break in a castle full of books, games and cousins—not to mention secret passages that came in handy during hide-and-seek. (Or when it was time to wash dishes.) It helped that all the Frumps were generous to a fault. Hazel and Ned hadn't packed for a long visit, so they were constantly having to borrow clothes, but no one complained. When Hazel couldn't even find the jacket and gloves she'd arrived with, Deirdre simply threw open her closet and told Hazel to help herself.

It was hard, of course, to say goodbye to their father, knowing they wouldn't see him again before the Christmas holidays. But they had two glorious days with him before he had to go, and Hazel got her voice back in time to issue strict instructions about his staying out of trouble and coming home safely, no matter what Interpol had in mind.

"Humph! You're a fine one to talk," Hazel's dad said. "Luckily, I have a plan to keep you kids out of trouble!"

It drove Hazel crazy that he wouldn't say anything more. Even though she and Ned were constantly finding their father and Charlotte in huddled conversations, they could never decipher their whispers. When Hazel demanded to know what they were plotting, her father gave his most mysterious smile and twirled an imaginary moustache.

"Just be sure to watch the mail for a very important letter, marked 'For Your Eyes Only'!"

The castle seemed a little empty after Colin Frump left, and even emptier once Mark and Matt returned to university—but Matt was only a ferry ride away, and liked to come home to do laundry. And Mark had his own mid-term break coming up and had promised to return and spend it with Hazel and Ned. Of course Deirdre and Oliver rushed home to see them each day after school, and most days Uncle Seamus left his office in Frontenac in time to join them for dinner. Even Charlotte dropped by most afternoons with funny tales of her veterinary work.

"But I think she's really just checking to see if we've got our letter yet," Ned confided to Hazel after a particularly brief visit.

In the meantime, Hazel had her history assignment. According to the e-mail from her teacher, Hazel was to imagine she lived from Confederation in 1867 to 1900. She should describe what her life was like and the changes she witnessed in Canada during those years.

That didn't sound too difficult. They'd covered some of that stuff in class, and Deirdre and Oliver obligingly checked out a small pile of reference books from their school library. Besides, history was a subject Hazel actually liked.

By the morning of Tuesday, October twenty-second, she had even made a few notes. Sitting in front of the enormous stone fireplace in the kitchen, listening to the hiss and crackle of the logs, Hazel closed her eyes. She imagined herself standing on the deck of one of the steamships that travelled the lakes and rivers of Canada in the late nineteenth century. It would be crowded and noisy and— Her reverie was interrupted by Ned's snort. She opened her eyes to see her brother waving a drawing of a woman in a long, puffy dress.

"Don't write about dopey stuff like this—clothes and food. Talk about the cool stuff."

"I will. I'm going to imagine I'm one of our ancestors travelling around the country," Hazel said. "That way I can talk about how the railroad was being built but people still used horses and buggies to get everywhere—and canoes in the backwoods."

"No, I'm talking about the *cool* stuff: like how we hadn't split the atom yet, or invented computers. Or airplanes. Or the space program . . ." Ned frowned. "Wait—you're supposed to pretend you're a typical person, living a typical life?"

Hazel nodded.

"Then you better pretend you're someone else's ancestor. Because ours built a castle. How typical is that?"

"Good point." Hazel chewed on the end of her pencil. "But I'd love to find out more about who lived here then—and those lost jewels."

Ned glanced at the grandfather clock in the corner of the room. "Hey—the mail should be here by now."

"Let's go."

Hazel and Ned had been walking down the long, tree-lined drive every morning to check for the letter. So far the mailbox had yielded nothing more interesting than a couple of cooking magazines addressed to Mark and a postcard from one of Oliver's friends.

"I'm glad it's not all slushy and muddy anymore," Ned said,

shuffling his feet through a mound of fallen leaves. "Maybe soon you'll feel up to shooting hoops."

"How about this afternoon, Squirt?"

"Seriously?"

Hazel nodded. She'd been feeling better every day, and now, nearly two weeks later, she had energy to burn. Besides, there was no way she was giving up that starting point guard job to Georgia Chandler. She planned to take advantage of this time to practise. The weather might be improving here, but it was still freezing in the northern part of the province where their schools were, and the power was out. The newspapers were full of stories about damage from the storm.

Hazel smiled to herself. There was no way their schools would reopen until November.

"Hey, Hazel, it's here! I've got it!"

Ned's tone was awestruck. He held out a thin, gold envelope, addressed to both of them in black, looping letters. Across the bottom were the words: *For Your Eyes Only*.

Hazel tore it open and with trembling fingers drew out two sheets of paper. Holding one so Ned could see, she read:

Come and find our hidden jewels,
Solve our riddles and follow our rules:
Neither uncle nor cousin may you consult
(The journey's as vital as the result).

So seek ye now the stones of birth;
Enjoy our game of skill and mirth.
These clues are simple, safe and fun,
By October's end you should be done!

Signed: Dad & Charlotte

Ned raised an eyebrow. "So Dad and Charlotte have made a treasure hunt? Like, with actual clues?"

"And actual treasure!" Hazel pointed to the line about the hidden jewels. "It sounds like we're looking for our birthstones."

"Big deal. I'd rather look for those lost jewels Deirdre talked about."

"But no one even knows if they exist! Besides, my birthstone's a ruby and yours is a sapphire, so . . . yeah, pretty big deal!"

"But why can't we consult Uncle Seamus and the cousins?" Ned crossed his arms over his chest. "That would be more fun."

"I guess because they know the castle so well. Dad must have thought that would make it too easy." Hazel sighed. "He doesn't seem to get how much we hate secrets."

She turned to the second sheet of paper. Across the top, the same looping hand had written: Clue #1. Hazel rolled her eyes.

"Thank goodness he labelled it. We'd never have guessed, otherwise."

Ned read aloud:

Today, my snowy breast is still,
The mice do what they may,
A pen was made from my old quill,
But the children have gone away.

Yet once I sailed far away,
Danced with a cat by the moon.
The voyage lasted a year and a day,
And we ate with a silly spoon.

For a few minutes neither of them spoke. Then Hazel carefully folded the papers again and slid them back into the envelope, and they slowly retraced their steps. At the top of the hill, Hazel broke the silence.

"Hey, Ned, porcupines have quills. Oh wait—they don't have snowy breasts."

When they reached the veranda, Ned smacked his forehead. "It's an owl."

"Of course!" Hazel felt silly for not seeing it sooner. "Owls hunt mice and you could make a quill pen out of their feathers."

But her excitement was dampened. If all the clues were this easy, it wouldn't be much of a treasure hunt. Their father had said they'd be done by the end of the month; at this rate they'd be done the whole thing by dinner!

Ned frowned. "I don't get all this other stuff, though—the sailing and the dancing. And what's with the silly spoon?"

"Actually, that part sounds familiar." But Hazel couldn't put her finger on why.

Inside the kitchen, Hazel placed the clue and the note side by side on the long wooden table. They stared at them for several minutes, but inspiration failed to strike.

"Right." Ned shrugged. "I'll use Oliver's computer to do some research. Maybe I can find some interesting scientific experiments that combine owls and dancing."

"You do that." Hazel opened the refrigerator and stared at its contents blindly. "I'm going to sit here and think. This clue reminds me . . . it's like there's something tugging at the back of my mind."

But whatever was tugging seemed to give up and slink away as she sat down in front of the fire, munching on Mark's homemade muffins and jam. Eventually Hazel stopped trying to remember and started flipping through her homework materials instead.

"Fenian Raids," she read aloud. "From the 1860s until the

1890s, many Canadians lived in fear of attack from a band of Americans called The Fenian Brotherhood. These Irish-Americans hoped to free Ireland from British rule, using Canada as hostage. From the battle of Ridgeway in 1866, the Fenian raids on Canadian forts, posts and villages never succeeded. But even though the invaders were beaten back, tensions remained high. In 1886, the British stationed warships at Vancouver, British Columbia, during the opening of the Canadian Pacific Railway, for fear of sabotage by the Fenians."

It's a good thing Canadians and Americans get along pretty well these days, Hazel reflected. The border was only a short boat ride away. She imagined herself in the nineteenth century. Would she lie awake at night worrying, wondering if a raiding party was already on its way, coming across the lake . . .?

"Hazel, do you know how much stuff there is on the Internet about owls?"

Ned's voice brought Hazel back to the present with a jerk.

"Uh, from the look on your face, I'm guessing lots?" she said.

Ned had a sheaf of paper in his arms. Hazel wondered if Oliver would need a new ink cartridge for his printer.

"Some of it's actually neat. Did you know there are schools that teach kids about the food chain by getting them to dissect regurgitated owl pellets? Little pellets of owl vomit! You get to pull out all the bones and stuff."

Hazel stared at Ned. He looked delighted. Not for the first time, she wondered how they could be related.

"Don't you think little kids would love that?" Ned didn't wait for her answer. "You know, I'm helping my science teacher with some of the younger grades this year and I'm totally going to bring this up with her when I get back to school. Get it? *Bring it up.*"

"Earth to Science Geek." Hazel waved a hand in Ned's face. "Did you happen to find out anything about the clue?"

Ned's face fell. He shuffled through his papers. "Well, there's over two hundred species of owl. And, uh, owls can represent, um . . . good luck, bad luck, wisdom, witches, death . . . Oh! I found this space experiment NASA was into, the Orbiting Wide-angle Light Collectors—get it? OWL? It has to do with observing high-energy cosmic rays from space."

Hazel held her head in her hands.

"Ned, do you honestly believe Dad has even *heard* about that stuff?"

"Sure."

Hazel glared at him.

"No . . . I guess not." Ned grinned. "But can I tell you about it anyway? It's seriously cool!"

"No." Hazel gritted her teeth. "It has nothing to do with the clue."

Ned shrugged and picked up the jars of jam. "Quince? What kind of flavour is quince? Is it related to mince—you know those mince pies Mark made for Thanksgiving?"

Hazel gasped. "Ned, you're a genius!"

"The preferred term these days is 'gifted,'" Ned said with a modest shrug.

"No, I remember now—it's a poem called 'The Owl and the Pussycat.' They dine on mince and slices of quince—which they ate with a spoon! I forget what kind of spoon exactly, but it was a made-up word . . . a runcible spoon?"

Ned placed his hand on her forehead.

"I think your fever's back," he said kindly.

Hazel swatted his hand away. "I'm talking about the clue, silly. It fits perfectly: in the poem, this owl and a cat. 'They sailed away for a year and a day' and 'They danced by the light of the moon.'"

"So are we looking for an owl, or for the poem about the owl?" Ned asked.

"I don't know—maybe both?"

"If it's a real owl, it must be dead. You know, *stuffed*." Ned pronounced the word with relish.

"Because the clue says its snowy breast is still? As in, not beating?" Hazel asked.

"Yeah. *Plus*, the clue says the mice are doing whatever they want. *Plus*, I don't think any owl is going to sit by and let you pluck out his quill to make a pen."

"A stuffed owl makes sense. One of the cousins could have made a pen using its quill—or even Dad or Uncle Seamus."

"Okay, so we're agreed." Ned looked at his watch. "We've still got tons of time before Deirdre and Oliver get home. Let's see if we can find a stuffed owl and, uh, something to do with this poem."

At Hazel's suggestion, they decided to split up, to conquer more territory. They agreed that Ned would take the east wing and Hazel the west wing. They were about to set off on their expeditions when Ned suddenly remembered the high-powered walkie-talkie set Uncle Seamus had sent him in September, for his tenth birthday. As he dashed off to retrieve the radios from the room he shared with Oliver, Hazel couldn't help rolling her eyes. "Walkie-talkies," she muttered. "Gimme a break."

But half an hour later, prowling through a dark, dusty corridor that couldn't have seen a human being in decades, Hazel was grateful for the gadgets. The castle was full of dim, unfamiliar rooms and nooks and crannies. Sometimes she found herself tiptoeing along creaking floorboards, trying not to hear the lonely cries of the wind. Sometimes she found herself padding silently on thick carpet in a room so still and forgotten, she was desperate for noise—any kind of noise. It was oddly reassuring to hear her brother's voice crackling over the airwaves.

"Come in, Hazel. Over."

"I'm here, Ned."

"You did it again! You're supposed to say 'Over.'"

"Over."

"No, you say it when you're done talking."

"Ha! Now *you* didn't say 'over'! Over."

"Hazel—whoa!"

"Tsk, tsk, Ned: you're not following the rules. You should have said 'Whoa *over*.' Over."

"I just found a stuffed buffalo head. Over."

"How many stuffed things does that make now? Over."

Ned sighed into the transmitter. "Lots. Somebody in this family sure loved to kill things. You found those snakes in the glass cases, and the rabbit. I found that stuffed eagle and a moose head, and a stuffed fox. Oh, and did I mention the bear? Over."

"Polar, grizzly, panda? Black?" Hazel paused.

"You're supposed to say '*over*.'" Ned almost yelled it.

"Sorry, I was still thinking of types of bears. It's pretty creepy. Hey, maybe we should put them all together in one room, like the ballroom, like some sort of Disney tableau gone bad. Over."

Ned didn't reply to that one. Hazel had reached the fourth floor now and was staring down a narrow hall so dark she couldn't see to the end. She flicked the light switch. Nothing happened.

She was awfully tempted to turn around and go back downstairs, but she'd been in scarier situations, and besides, she was curious.

"Come in, Ned. Over."

"Why are you whispering? I can't hear if you whisper. Over."

"Sorry. I'm on the fourth floor and the lights don't work. But I'm going to check it out anyway. Over."

As Hazel's eyes adjusted to the gloom, she began to wish

they hadn't. The windowless corridor was lined with doors on either side. And between the doors stood things she thought at first were statues. But as she crept closer, Hazel could see that they weren't. Ned hadn't been kidding when he'd said somebody in their family had liked to kill things.

To Hazel's left, a black bear reared up, its jaw fixed in a ferocious snarl. She swallowed. On the opposite side of the corridor two stuffed wolves appeared to be dancing on their hind legs. Up ahead she could see some kind of waterfowl, also posed as if dancing, teetering on spindly legs.

"There's got to be an owl here someplace," she muttered.

By the time Hazel reached the end of the corridor, she'd seen all sorts of stuffed birds and animals frozen in strange dancelike poses, sometimes in pairs, some performing solo. But no owl.

As she retraced her steps, Hazel forced herself to turn the knob of each door and peek inside. And every time, she felt as if something was waiting there, ready to jump out at her. Many of the doors groaned horribly—their hinges obviously hadn't been used much in this century—but most revealed empty rooms. Eventually Hazel found a room used for storage; in the dim light, even the cardboard boxes and wooden packing crates took on a sinister air. She jumped as the walkie-talkie, forgotten in her hand, sputtered to life.

"Come in, Hazel. Over."

"Oh, Ned—you startled me! This place is truly weird. Wait until you see it. Uh, over."

"Uh-huh. So, I found a couple of stuffed owls, but no clue. Listen, I've been thinking: we never solved the part about the children being gone away. Over."

"Ned, I think *I* need to go away. It's totally dark up here and I feel like if I turn around, I'll find out that I'm being followed by all these freaky dead animals. And now I sort of wish I hadn't said that out loud. Over."

"Hazel, stop babbling and listen. Shouldn't there be an old schoolroom around here somewhere? Remember Uncle Seamus telling us he and Dad were like the first generation to get to go to school in the village?"

Hazel was about to reply, when she heard a sound behind her. She froze. It was like being in a nightmare, when you know you should turn around, but are too scared to move. Taking a deep breath, she forced herself to look. The door across the hall was ajar. And the corridor suddenly felt cold.

In that split second, undecided whether to scream or run, Hazel remembered that the room she had just checked had a broken window. Relief flooded through her—the draft had opened the door.

Smiling to herself, she crossed the hall, intending to take a quick look beyond the open door and then get the heck out of there. But what she saw inside that last room made her stop dead.

"Ned? Come in, Ned—I just found the old schoolroom! Over."

"Are you sure? Over."

Hazel stepped farther into the room. A dusty globe sat atop an adult-sized desk that faced half a dozen smaller desks arranged in rows. Strange maps hung on the walls and leather-bound books lined the shelves across the back of the room.

"Ned? I'm sure. And—yikes!"

"What? The owl? Over."

"No, a skeleton. I just backed into a skeleton. Never mind, I'm sure it's just a plastic model. Over."

"Cool! It's probably real—they used to use real bones, a long time ago. Does it look old? Over."

"You know what, Ned? Why don't *you* come on up here and take a look at it? Over."

"I'm on my way. If you find the clue before I get there, don't open it, okay? Over."

"I promise. Uh, over."

Heavy black curtains hung across the far wall. Hazel yanked them open and enormous, choking clouds of dust rose into the air. After she'd stopped coughing, she decided it had been worth it. Now she could truly survey her surroundings. In a dim corner, partially hidden by a bookcase and a suit of armour, a gigantic snowy owl stared balefully back at her.

She'd only sworn not to *open* the clue before Ned arrived; he didn't say she couldn't *look* for it. But as she drew closer, Hazel wasn't sure she even wanted to touch the enormous bird. Battered yet majestic, it sat under a blanket of dust and a lacy veil of cobwebs; surely no one had touched it for years.

Tucking the walkie-talkie in her pocket, Hazel poked at the owl gingerly. Nothing. She lifted it carefully with both hands. No paper or envelope tucked under its wing. Now what? Her eyes flickered over the rest of the shelf. Everything was covered in the same thick layer of dust. Except . . . her heart leapt. A suspiciously dust-free book with a binding of blue paper had been inserted into the array of ancient leather-bound volumes. Hazel pulled out the book and peered at the cover: *The Nonsense Poems of Edward Lear.* Yes, that was the name of the poet who'd written "The Owl and the Pussycat"!

She held the book upside down and shook it gently. A thin silver envelope dropped to the floor. Victory!

As she bent to retrieve it, Hazel stumbled, falling against the suit of armour. Grabbing hold of the battle-axe by its handle, she managed to regain her footing for a moment. But only a moment.

She heard a *click*, and the axe shifted under her grip. With a terrible groan, the stone floor beneath her feet slid away, and suddenly Hazel was dangling above a dark abyss. For a sickening moment, she clung to the axe, her feet scrabbling for purchase. Then her hand slipped. And she was tumbling down, down, down into the inky blackness below.

CHAPTER FOUR

"Jinxed!" Hazel practically spat out the word, along with a mouthful of dust and a few drops of blood. She'd bitten her tongue on the way down.

Incredibly, that seemed to be her worst injury. She'd have a few bruises later, and there were several painful splinters in her right hand from her attempt to grab onto a wooden ladder she'd bumped against. But that was it. What had saved her, Hazel realized now, was a mattress. She was lying on a thick mattress at the bottom of a ladder. And that was all she could be sure of; it was too dark to see much beyond her outstretched arm.

"Hazel?" Ned's voice sounded miles away. She hadn't fallen that far! But, of course, Ned didn't know what room she was in. He was probably somewhere in the hall, getting spooked by all the stuffed dead creatures.

"I'm here," Hazel hollered. She reached into her pocket for the walkie-talkie, but it wasn't there. It must have tumbled out when she fell.

Hazel squinted at the opening above her. That battle-axe

she'd grabbed must be a lever, connected somehow to the gear that had swung open the floor. But if the floor could be opened accidentally, could it close accidentally? The air was musty, dank and suddenly difficult to breathe. The darkness pressed in on her. The last thing she wanted was to be stuck down here with the trap door shut and no way to explain to Ned how to open it again. She started to climb.

Hazel was almost at the top when she heard the *click*.

"No!" she screamed. It was too late. Above her head, just out of reach, the stone panel slid back into place, blotting out the light. She was trapped.

Hazel froze, one foot on a ladder rung, the other poised in mid-climb. Where was Ned? He had to be coming—how long could it take him to find the schoolroom? Maybe she should yell again—would he hear her through the stone? Slowly, Hazel edged up to the next rung on the ladder, and then the next. Then she stopped. If the walkie-talkie had survived the fall, it could be the key to getting out of here.

Hazel retraced her steps until she reached the bottom. She felt around the edges of the mattress. Nothing. Telling herself there was no reason to be frightened, that she would be out of here in no time, Hazel got down on her hands and knees and started crawling around on the stone floor beside the mattress. There! The tip of her finger brushed against the walkie-talkie.

"Ned, are you there? Over." Hazel waited. No response. She hoped the transmitter was working. "Ned, come in. Come in, Ned."

"Where are you? Over."

Hazel realized she had been holding her breath. She let it out now in a gusty sigh. "Ned, please tell me you're in the schoolroom. Over."

"Yes. And I see the owl, but I don't see you. Wait a second—I just found the clue on the floor! Hazel, what's going on? Over."

"Ned, I'm right underneath you. I'm trapped in, like, a dungeon or something. Over."

"How can you have an upstairs dungeon? Over."

"Just get me out of here! There's a secret trap door and you open it by pulling on the battle-axe—part of the suit of armour. It should be right in front of you. Do you see it? Over."

There was a burst of static after Hazel finished speaking, but no reply. She shook the transmitter helplessly, wondering whether Ned had heard all of her instructions.

Then, the sound she most wanted to hear—the grinding of a gear as the stone above her head slid back, revealing her brother's worried face.

"I don't think we should split up anymore," Ned said as he helped her through the opening. "It's not efficient. Not if one of us has to go rescuing the other."

A horrid thought occurred to Hazel. "On the other hand, what if we'd been together? Both of us could be trapped down there and no one would know!"

Ned's eyes widened behind his glasses. Then he gave himself a little shake and said briskly, "We'd just have rescued ourselves. Somehow. C'mon, let's get out of here."

Hazel was relieved to return to the familiar parts of the castle. When they reached the main floor, she started to giggle.

"Hang on a sec, Ned. What did Dad and Charlotte say? The clues are 'simple, safe and fun'?"

They were both laughing as they entered the kitchen to find Charlotte, Deirdre and Oliver in the middle of preparing dinner.

"Where were you guys?" Oliver said. "I looked all over for you."

"We were hunting owls," Ned said.

"And nearly got caught in a trap ourselves," Hazel added.

"Oh, the letter came!" Charlotte clapped her hands. "Finally—you can start the treasure hunt!"

"What treasure hunt?" Deirdre and Oliver said at the same time.

Hazel and Ned exchanged confused glances. Wasn't this supposed to be a secret?

But Charlotte nodded to them, smiling. "Oh, go ahead, we didn't say you couldn't tell them about it. We just said you couldn't ask for help. But what did you say about a trap?"

Charlotte's smile faded when she heard about the strange, dungeonlike room. It turned out none of the Frumps knew of its existence. Of course, Deirdre and Oliver wanted to see for themselves straightaway. But Charlotte insisted on removing Hazel's splinters first and bandaging her hand.

When they reached the fourth floor, Hazel decided the dead, oddly posed animals that lined the corridor didn't seem half so creepy now. It helped to have reinforcements—not to mention powerful flashlights.

Charlotte made them all stand clear when she pulled the battle-axe to open the trap door. Oliver complained that he could see nothing from his vantage point on top of a desk several feet away.

"That's as close as you're going to get." Charlotte peered into the darkness. "It's bad enough that Hazel got hurt solving the first clue of what was supposed to be a perfectly safe treasure hunt! I'm not letting you down there until Seamus gets home."

"We could take turns," Deirdre said. "One of us could stay up here to work the axe-lever thingy, in case the trap door closes again."

"What if the lever breaks?"

"We could jam something across the opening, so that it can't close," Ned said.

After several more minutes of arguing, an iron curtain rod was found and wedged across the opening. But Charlotte remained in the schoolroom as the four Frumps, flashlights in hand, descended the ladder.

"There's nothing here." Deirdre's disappointment showed in her voice. "No furniture, nothing. Just this old mattress."

"There's a door over here, but it's locked." Ned jiggled the knob.

"It's kind of spooky. Did you notice there are no windows?" Oliver said. He directed the beam of his flashlight along the stone walls. When he spoke again, his voice was so faint, Hazel had to strain to hear the words. "Why would anyone make a room with no windows?"

"Maybe it was a darkroom—you know, for developing photographs?" Deirdre said.

"Maybe." Hazel led the way back up the ladder. "But photography wasn't that common as a hobby back when this castle was built. I was just reading about that for my history assignment. The first really popular camera that everybody bought was the Brownie, and it didn't come out until 1900."

Charlotte inspected the room next, but she didn't take long.

"I'm so sorry this happened, Hazel," she said as she re-emerged through the opening, "but nobody even knew this room existed."

"That door I found must lead to the third-floor hallway." Ned frowned. "I don't remember seeing a door there."

As they galumphed down the stairs, Hazel found herself wondering about the animals. There was a word for that—*taxi*-something . . . *taxidermy!* Could the secret room have been a workshop for the taxidermist? But surely any hobby involving chemicals and dead animals was one you'd want to do in a room with windows. *Open* windows.

When they reached the third floor, they realized why none of them had stumbled across the secret room before. The third-floor door was nowhere to be seen. It was completely hidden behind a bookcase that stretched from floor to ceiling.

"Ooh, do you think there's a button somewhere that we press to open the door?" As she spoke, Deirdre began pressing on the wooden shelves and pulling out books to peer behind for a mechanism that would move the shelf. Hazel joined her. But Oliver shone his flashlight into the gap between the bookcase and the wall.

"I can see the door, and it's not attached to the bookcase or anything. Somebody just put the bookcase in front of it."

"Well, we don't need to start moving bookcases around, considering we've already seen the room." Charlotte's tone was no-nonsense. "Besides, it's time for dinner."

As they made their way back down to the kitchen, Ned motioned to Hazel to hang back behind the others.

"We forgot all about the clue—it's still in my pocket." Ned handed Hazel the envelope. "Here—you found it first. You open it."

This one was written in the same black, looping hand as the first clue, and labelled Clue #2. Hazel held it so they could both read:

My name is a word that means: forgive;
In the nineteenth century I did live.
Seek me now in a place of quiet thought,
Among ancestors ye have long forgot.

"Interesting." Ned stroked his chin. "At least it doesn't say we have to go at night."

"What are you talking about?" Hazel stared at him. "Go where at night?"

Ned shrugged.

"Isn't it obvious? It's a cemetery!"

CHAPTER FIVE

"**M**an, I'm good." Ned oozed satisfaction. "What would you do without me?"

"Oh, I'd find some way to cope." Hazel dumped the breakfast dishes into the sink. "Listen, I couldn't fall asleep last night—I was thinking so hard about the clue. What if it's not a cemetery? What if it's a monastery? That's a place of quiet thought. Or it could be a library, or a study hall."

Ned snorted.

They'd been arguing since yesterday. Part of Hazel knew that she was resisting Ned's solution precisely because it was Ned's— and because he'd solved it so irritatingly fast. But another part of her simply didn't want the clue to be in a cemetery. It wasn't that she found cemeteries spooky; she found them sad. Once she'd tried to describe to Mark the way they made her feel, the loneliness at the pit of her stomach. He'd called it melancholy. Whatever it was, Hazel wasn't in the mood for it today.

Deirdre and Oliver had the day off school—some kind of professional development day for teachers. Uncle Seamus had taken Deirdre across to Frontenac on the ferry; she was to spend the day shopping and having lunch with friends, while

Uncle Seamus was at work. Hazel could have gone along, but Deirdre's friends, although nice, didn't seem to have much in common with Hazel. Unless shopping involved vintage NBA jerseys (she'd been looking for an Alvin Williams #20 for a while) or the latest in basketball shoes, Hazel wasn't interested. So now she was left trying to wriggle her way out of exploring village graveyards with Ned and Oliver. Technically, of course, Oliver wasn't going to be searching for Frump headstones— that would be *helping*. But the boys had decided that riding their bikes together wasn't helping. And once they reached the village, if Oliver happened to take Ned past the two cemeteries, and Ned happened to stop and take a look around, well, that wasn't helping either. Oliver would have to stay with Ned, for politeness' sake, but he certainly wouldn't *help*.

Hazel wasn't at all sure she should let the boys go on their own. Uncle Seamus hadn't been too pleased about her tumble into the secret room. He wasn't angry at her, of course, but after he'd inspected the room for himself, he had asked to see the clues, shaken his head and sighed. Then he'd looked at Charlotte and said in his most lawyerlike voice that he certainly hoped the rest of the clues would live up to their promise to be safe, and not lead to danger.

"Earth to Hazel!" Ned snapped his fingers under her nose. "Did you hear me? I said, before we go, we still need to figure out whose grave we're supposed to be looking for."

Hazel nodded. They'd been unable to come up with another word for *forgive*. It was time to consult the enormous dictionary that—for no reason the cousins had ever been able to explain— resided in the kitchen.

With exaggerated care, Hazel turned the yellowed pages. Each was as thin as a tissue and as brittle as a dried leaf. It would be a miracle if she didn't tear one.

"'Forgive,'" she read aloud. "'To give or grant, to pardon an offence or an offender.'"

"Grant!" Ned punched the air in triumph. "Yes! All we need is the tombstone for Mr. Grant Frump, and Clue #3 will be ours!"

He rubbed his hands together and gave his best imitation of a maniacal laugh. Hazel frowned.

"How can you be so sure it's that simple?"

"First, there's a kid at school named Grant, so I know it's a real name. Second, have you ever heard of someone named Pardon? Think about it—it's a comedy skit waiting to happen!"

Hazel looked at him blankly.

Sighing, Ned launched into a mock dialogue: "Hi, I'm Joe— What's your name? *Uh, Pardon.* I said, what's your name? *Pardon.* Et cetera, et cetera . . . It ends with poor old Pardon getting slugged by Joe. And then suing the parents who named him."

Hazel laughed in spite of herself.

Oliver bounded into the room, two bike helmets swinging from his hands, his forehead creased with worry.

"Hazel, I can't find a helmet for you. Deirdre's must be around here someplace, but I can't find it!"

"That's okay." Hazel paused. This was the perfect excuse. "You guys can go without me."

"I thought we decided we wouldn't split up anymore," Ned said.

"True—but you won't be alone, you'll have Oliver."

"*I'm* never the one we need to worry about," Ned pointed out.

Hazel smiled. "Tell you what—I promise that I'll work on my history assignment and nothing else. And you promise that if you find Grant Frump, you won't peek at Clue #3! Deal?"

They shook hands solemnly. Then Hazel settled into one of the armchairs by the hearth and began sifting through her pile of notes. A chill breeze swirled through the kitchen as the door closed behind the boys, but she hardly noticed, as she burrowed deeper into the nineteenth century.

"In 1866, more than eight hundred American troops crossed the Niagara River to seize the town of Fort Erie in a surprise attack. Telegraph and rail lines were damaged, and the town fell almost instantly. The Fenian flag was hoisted, and for awhile it fluttered above the town. But when no reinforcements arrived from the United States, British soldiers and Canadian volunteers were able to beat back the invaders."

The Fenians didn't seem to have support from their own country for their raids, Hazel reflected. They were like badly behaving kids whose parents ignore them as long as possible. But people died in the battles, at Fort Erie and in other attacks, too, out west and on the east coast. And wasn't some politician assassinated by Fenians? She flipped through the pages of one of the books Deirdre had brought her. Yes—there it was, one of the Fathers of Confederation, Thomas D'Arcy McGee, shot dead on his front steps after a late-night meeting of Parliament. McGee had spoken out against the Fenians and urged the government to organize a militia of Canadians, train them to defend the country against more attacks. He was murdered in 1868. By the 1870s, tens of thousands of Canadians had joined the militia.

The flames were dying down. Soon there would be nothing left on the hearth but glowing embers. She should add a log. It would be much cozier to hear the cheerful hiss and crackle of burning wood than the wind outside, moaning. Such a mournful, lonely sound—like crying. Like the girl in her dream: *What has he done?*

Hazel hugged herself. The girl could have been lamenting a brother or a father who'd run off to join the militia. Or even the Fenians.

Enough of this. The fighting and fear and loss was in the

past. This history assignment was in the present. Hazel sat up straighter. There was work to do, and a perfectly good library in the south tower where she could do it!

But the castle had never seemed quite so empty, and the hallways had never seemed so long or so deserted. Despite its thick stone walls, Land's End was anything but silent; pipes rumbled in the basement, and the glass in the windows rattled, as if the lonely wind were knocking, trying to get in.

It took more determination than Hazel had expected to push open the heavy oak door and quickly scan the perfectly round room, with its carved wooden bookcases that reached all the way up to the two-storey ceiling. But this was no dream; there was no fire in the hearth and no weeping girl. Hazel took a deep breath and stepped inside.

Entering the library was like stepping back in time: no computers, only long wooden tables flanked by narrow, upright chairs with cracked leather upholstery. To reach the uppermost books on the first floor, there were oak ladders that slid along on narrow brass railings. As for the books on the second level, a spiral staircase led to a catwalk that encircled the room. The room was dim; no light seemed to come through the stained glass windows in the domed ceiling. Hazel glanced at the hanging light fixtures. They looked so ancient she figured they couldn't possibly work, but a flick of the switch bathed the room in a warm light that was almost welcoming. Here and there the shelves of books were interrupted by dusty oil paintings of men and women in old-fashioned clothes.

Hazel peered closer at one painting. It depicted a white-haired man, with a slightly sinister smile, dressed in a long black coat and holding a gold pocket watch. He was standing in a room full of books. On the wall behind him was some sort of sign or plaque. Hazel squinted. The sign read: VERITAS. That was the Latin word for truth, wasn't it? Her eye caught a title on the gold plate affixed to the bottom of the frame: EDWIN CORNELIUS FRUMP, 1871. Creepy. She was related to that guy?

Hazel turned away. On the opposite wall a cheerier painting depicted an elderly woman dressed in a long gown. She was sewing by the light of a window. Hazel crossed the room to take a better look. The nameplate read: MERCY FRUMP.

Hazel's heart thudded against her chest. *Mercy* Frump? *Mercy* was pretty close to *forgive*.

She whirled around. There were dozens of portraits. With trembling legs, she moved toward another painting. SHEELAGH FRUMP. DEIRDRE FRUMP. FERGUS FRUMP. Hazel was surrounded by ancestors. Long-forgotten ancestors?

Gingerly, Hazel reached behind the edges of the painting of Mercy and felt along the frame. Something fluttered to the floor—a tiny silver envelope with blue writing. Without thinking of Ned, Hazel opened the flap and took out the clue.

"He clasps the crag with crooked hands;
Close to the sun in lonely lands."
But he's not stuffed—he's made of stone;
He's inside and outside—all alone.

Hazel sighed. Their father had better make the next clue about math or science, something Ned would enjoy! She stared at the portrait of Mercy.

"Were you a poetry person? Not me. I like novels . . . and books about basketball." Hazel contemplated Mercy's gown. "You probably never played basketball—it wasn't even invented until 1891. A Canadian guy made it up, you know, but he was living in the United States at the time. I guess that whole Fenian crisis was over by then."

Hazel decided to set aside Clue #3 until Ned returned, and go back to her history assignment. But it was hard to know where to begin. The books were shelved with a reckless disregard for the Dewey Decimal system. After some time spent wandering around the room, plucking books from shelves, Hazel had an armful of dusty but hopeful-sounding titles like *Farming on Île du Loup*, *A Genealogy of Frontenac* and *Life in Upper Canada*. She plunked herself down on the worn Persian carpet and began to read.

Some of the information was useful; Hazel jotted down notes. In the late nineteenth century, food sounded cheap—a whole turkey for a dollar and fifty cents? But a factory worker might toil ten hours a day, six days a week, for as little as five dollars a week.

Still, many of the books were downright boring. After a while, Hazel's eyes started to glaze over. Eventually, in the middle of a gigantic yawn, she realized she'd been reading the same page over and over. Setting down the book, Hazel stretched her legs out in front of her and waggled her toes, pushing against the high wooden baseboard where the floor and wall met. There was a *click*, and part of the baseboard swung inward, revealing a hidey-hole.

"Hey!" Flipping over onto her belly, Hazel peered into the hole. The opening wasn't big enough to see anything except inky blackness. But she couldn't *not* explore it. Hazel examined the baseboard. She hadn't broken anything—it was cleverly, almost invisibly hinged. Someone had designed this as a hiding place, probably when the castle was first built. Maybe it was still hiding something.

Pushing aside thoughts of creepy-crawly creatures, Hazel thrust her arm into the opening.

Nothing. She reached deeper, her hand fanning across the floorboards until her arm had disappeared up to the elbow. Still nothing. But—had her fingertip just brushed something smooth? It had corners—so whatever it was, it wasn't alive. Hazel edged closer and thrust her arm inside, all the way up to the shoulder. Gotcha! She grabbed the object and pulled it out.

A book.

Hazel sneezed. A very dusty book.

She was already up to her ears in books. And dust. But this book was different. The pages looked as if they'd been cut by hand and sewn together. And they were handwritten.

Was it a diary?

In Hazel's experience, most diaries just proved that life was boring and nothing ever happened. She had tried to keep a diary herself—several times. It never worked out. She'd start by writing every day, then slide into once a week, then once a month. She'd reread her entries, finding each one more tedious than the last. Endless descriptions of what she'd eaten for dinner or the basketball drills she'd practised with her best friend, Alysha.

"But this could really help me with my history assignment." Hazel turned the book over in her hands. "Especially if it belonged to one of my ancestors."

She opened the book, expecting to see the name of the diary's owner. Instead she found a sketch of a hawk. Her pulse jumped. A hawk? That reminded her of something . . . Hazel still hadn't been able to recall the details of her trek through the storm, but suddenly she *knew* there had been something about a hawk. If only she could remember . . .

As she bent to examine the drawing more closely, a gust of cold air swept over her, as if someone had just opened the door to the library. The pages of the book fluttered. She looked up to see who had come in, but the door was still closed and the room still empty.

Hazel glanced down at the book again. The breeze had left it open at the title page. She read it in disbelief: "*My Book of Spells and Magicks.*"

CHAPTER SIX

Recipe for Removing Heartache

Take one cup of water from a hidden stream,
Two grains of sand from a forgotten shore,
Three whiskers of a blind field mouse,
Four leaves of tansy,
Five tears from a remorseful child.
Mix by starlight and sprinkle over doorstep before dawn.

"Seriously?" Hazel said.

The book was filled with spells and cures. Her eyes skimmed over instructions for getting rid of warts, stuttering and blindness. Some of the spells looked more like recipes, with ingredients found in most kitchens. Others called for herbs Hazel had never heard of and stuff that made no sense. Tears from a remorseful child? Mouse whiskers?

Somewhere a clock struck four. Hazel jumped. Ned and Oliver should be arriving home soon, not to mention Uncle Seamus and Deirdre.

Hazel bit her lip. Ned! First, she'd found the clue without him and broken their agreement about reading it together.

Second, she'd discovered a secret hiding place and a book of spells! If their places were reversed, she'd be miffed. Hazel thought for a moment. There was no sense pretending not to have read the clue—she'd ripped open the envelope. But if she replaced the magic book in its hiding place, she could bring Ned back here and let him open the secret door for himself . . .

Hazel stuffed the clue in her pocket, tucked the book back into the hidden compartment and gently nudged the baseboard until it clicked shut. The pile of books she'd gathered for the history assignment, she left on one of the tables. On her way out, she flicked off the lights. But at the threshold, she froze.

She was being watched. A pair of eyes bored into the back of her skull.

Hazel wheeled around.

The room was empty. But in the dim light, the pale, leering face of Edwin Cornelius Frump seemed to glow. For a moment Hazel stared at it, paralyzed, before turning on her heel. As she ran, she told herself it wasn't fear; she was just anxious to find Ned. Or anyone from this century.

Rounding the corner on the main floor, Hazel nearly hurtled headlong into Deirdre, laden with shopping bags, on the way to her room.

"Whoa!" Deirdre flattened herself against the nearest wall, crushing an antique tapestry. "Where are you going in such a hurry?"

"Sorry." Hazel stopped, panting. "I was just . . . it's nothing, actually. I guess I just got a little spooked, being here alone."

"No worries." Deirdre picked up a bag she'd dropped as she sprang out of Hazel's way. "You're not alone anymore, anyway. Dad's in his study, and I passed Ned and Oliver a second ago, on their way to Oliver's room. Do you want to see what I bought?"

"Uh, sure. Maybe later? I just have to find Ned." Hazel bounded up the staircase.

Ned slept in Oliver's tower room whenever they visited. It had once been a magnificent space, with its high ceilings and elaborate stone carvings around the Gothic windows. But Oliver had given over much of his room to a chemistry lab and a robotics workshop. Unintelligible charts and diagrams covered much of the walls and floor.

The boys were stretched out across Oliver's sofa, lying toe to toe. Hazel thought for a moment they were asleep, but Ned opened one eye.

"We're beat. What a complete and total waste of time." Ned closed his eye again and slumped even deeper into the sofa. "We went to three cemeteries and didn't find any Frumps. What's the deal with that?"

"Maybe our ancestors had some weird tradition, like burial at sea." Oliver's voice was muffled because he'd turned his face into the cushions. "It's nice and warm in here, isn't it?"

"Sure." Hazel perched on the arm of the sofa closest to Ned. "Uh, so . . . it turns out the quiet place wasn't a cemetery any-way— it was the library. And it wasn't Grant Frump we were looking for, it was Mercy Frump."

She dug the clue out of her pocket and placed it in Ned's palm. "Here you go."

Ned's eyes flew open. "What? You're kidding me!"

As Ned and Oliver stared at the clue, Hazel explained about the portrait.

"I found something else kind of strange too, but I put it back so you can see for yourself. Come on."

But Ned was still looking at the clue. He shook his head slightly and turned to Oliver.

"Hey, can I use your computer for a second? I need to check something."

Oliver nodded. Intrigued, Hazel tipped a pile of smelly socks, sweaters and underwear from a chair so she could sit beside Ned and watch what he did on the Internet.

"See this part here, that's in quotation marks?" Ned pointed to the clue.

"'He clasps the crag with crooked hands; close to the sun in lonely lands,'" Hazel read aloud. "Yeah, I noticed that."

"Well, it sounds really familiar. I think it's from a poem I had to memorize for school last year. If we type in the whole quote, including the quotation marks, the search engine should be able to find the poem."

Ned finished typing and hit Enter. In seconds, the computer screen filled with hits. Ned clicked on the first one, and read aloud:

He clasps the crag with crooked hands;
Close to the sun in lonely lands,
Ring'd with the azure world, he stands.

The wrinkled sea beneath him crawls;
He watches from his mountain walls,
And like a thunderbolt he falls.

"What does it mean?" Oliver had joined them now and was staring at the computer monitor. Ned scrolled down the screen.

"It's called 'The Eagle,'" he said. "And it's by Alfred, Lord Tennyson."

"Oh. It's about an *eagle*." Hazel could sort of see that now. "I think I've heard of Lord Alfred Tennyson."

Ned sighed. "No. It's Alfred, Lord Tennyson. Don't ask me why the Lord part comes after his first name, it just does. Anyway, I don't think it matters who the poet is."

"There's a stuffed eagle in the basement," Oliver offered. "Oh, sorry. I'm not supposed to help."

Ned grimaced. "Of course there is. What is it with this place and stuffed dead things, anyway?"

Hazel shook her head. "The clue says right at the start that we're not looking for a stuffed eagle—this one's made of stone."

"Hey!" Deirdre leaned against the door jamb. "It's dinnertime, you guys."

Throughout the meal, and even as she sat in Deirdre's room later that evening applauding her cousin's purchases, Hazel's mind was puzzling over the rest of the clue. How could the stone eagle be inside and outside at the same time? Nothing came to her.

"Hey, did you hear me?" Deirdre snapped her fingers in front of Hazel's face "I said, I ran into Hank Packham in Frontenac today. He wanted me to tell you he made the basketball team this year, and he was hoping you'd have time to practise with him, before your school reopens."

"Oh. Uh, sure." To her annoyance, Hazel felt her cheeks grow warm. Hank was a boy Hazel had met last summer. They'd gotten off to a rocky start, when he and Kenny Pritchard and a third boy, Billy, had challenged Hazel, Ned and Oliver to a game of three-on-three that had turned violent. But eventually, Hazel and Hank had become friends. Good friends. She'd been wondering if she'd have a chance to see him.

"The only problem is, Hank was on his way to the train station." Deirdre frowned at her reflection in the mirror. "He's gone to visit some relatives, but he said he hoped to be back in time for the big Halloween party next week.

"What big Halloween party?"

"I'll pick up one of the flyers they have in town so you can read all about it. They do a costume party over at the pioneer village every year. You'll love it. Tons of candy, bobbing for apples. They open up most of the buildings so kids and even adults can trick-or-treat."

"Sounds . . . different," Hazel said.

"It's a little wild but fun. I think I've still got the costume I wore last year. Let me show you . . ."

It was a frustrating night. Hazel escaped Deirdre's fashion show as soon as she politely could, but any hope of bringing Ned back to the library to show him the hidden spell book was dashed by the arrival of Charlotte, a dazzling new computer game in her hands. There was no competing with The Archaeologist's Doom—and the hours until bedtime were filled with Egyptian pharaohs, explorers and mercenaries, not to mention extreme curses, booby-trapped temples and hit points.

Later, lying in bed, Hazel's brain buzzed with a jumble of images: Fenians, Egyptians, sphinxes and eagles. When she closed her eyes, she could still see the game, with the walls of the archaeologist's dig and the chambers of the excavated pyramid.

"Oh." Hazel sat bolt upright. "Walls—that's it! That's how you can be inside and outside at the same time!"

Tossing back the covers, she paused just long enough to shove her feet into slippers and grab a sweatshirt. The halls between her room and the boys' tower seemed extra dark and filled with shadows, but she was determined to tell Ned she'd solved the clue.

Oliver was deep in sleep when Hazel slipped into the room, but she could see a flashlight under Ned's covers. Reading again? She crept up as noiselessly as she could, and yanked the blankets away. Ned jumped, knocking his chemistry textbook to the floor.

"Hey!" Ned shone the flashlight's beam directly into her laughing eyes.

"Shhh—and point that someplace else!" Hazel turned away, shielding her face.

"What are you doing here?" Ned lowered the beam, but not his voice.

"Shhh—you'll wake Oliver," Hazel whispered. "I solved the clue."

"Oh." Ned sat up, adjusting his spectacles. "Okay."

"Remember the walled garden, on the east side of the castle grounds? I think we're looking for a stone statue of an eagle in that garden. *Inside* the stone walls, but *outside* the castle—you know, outdoors."

"That could fit."

"Could? It's perfect—it doesn't get more perfect than that!"

"There's no such thing as *more* perfect," Ned said, hunting for his slippers. "That's like saying something is more unique, or more dead."

Hazel ground her teeth, but "Bring the flashlight" was all she said.

Yet, as they crept downstairs, Hazel found herself questioning the wisdom of exploring the garden by night. They had only the one flashlight, and it was a big garden. They might not be able to spot the statue, let alone the clue. By the time they opened the kitchen door and stepped out onto the veranda, she was convinced this was a very bad idea. Night had brought with it a cold, damp wind, and inky clouds blotted out the moon and stars. They couldn't see the walled garden from the veranda—it lay on the other side of the castle. From here they could only gaze upon the mass of gnarled, twisted branches that looked nothing like the cheerful orchard of daytime. Beyond the sinister, creaking trees lay the waters of Lake Ontario, cold, black and forbidding.

"Aw, let's wait until tomorrow," Ned said. "It's not like the clue's going anywhere."

"Well, if you insist."

But when they reached the hall where their paths separated, Ned shone his flashlight at Hazel's face again.

"Quit that!" She batted the light away.

"Sorry—but listen, as long as we're up, why don't you show me the thing you found in the library?"

Hazel nodded. She was wide awake, and by the look of him, so was Ned. But as they padded down the hallway, their slippers silent on the Persian carpet, Hazel contemplated the library at night. The image of Edwin Cornelius Frump's leering portrait jumped into her mind. She told herself sternly that there was nothing to fear, but when they reached the oak door and she placed her hand on the cold brass doorknob, she felt her stomach flutter.

"What are you waiting for?" Ned asked.

She turned the knob.

Hazel's first thought was that the clouds must have cleared, because the room was flooded with moonlight. Illuminated in this ghostly manner, Edwin Cornelius Frump seemed almost to lean out of his ornate picture frame. Hazel swallowed; she could have sworn his smile was twisted into a malicious grin.

"Wow." Ned's voice was small. "I never noticed how creepy that painting is."

"Uh-huh." Hazel felt along the wall for the light switch. "Maybe I'll just turn on the lights."

But this time when she flicked the switch, nothing happened.

"Old wiring," Ned said in a still smaller voice. "Uncle Seamus should really have that looked at."

The hidey-hole was on the side of the library facing Edwin's portrait. Somehow, even with her brother at her side, Hazel couldn't bring herself to turn her back on the painting. Feeling slightly foolish, she grabbed Ned and began sidling along the wall, keeping her eyes on the portrait and her back against the bookshelves, Hazel used her foot to feel along the baseboard behind her.

"This is it, Ned. There's a secret compartment in the baseboard. Just push here."

Click. Hazel heard the baseboard open. She kept her eyes on the spooky painting as Ned reached into the opening.

"There's nothing there," Ned said. Now his voice sounded suspicious, as if Hazel might be playing some kind of trick.

"Just reach deeper. Don't worry—it's nothing slimy or disgusting."

"Uh-huh. You get it, then."

With an exasperated sigh, Hazel knelt down and reached inside the compartment. Odd. The book should be right here. She reached her hand in deeper. Nothing.

The secret compartment was empty. Hazel glanced up, stunned.

From across the room, Edwin Cornelius Frump grinned.

CHAPTER SEVEN

"Is this some kind of joke?" Ned asked. His voice faltered on the word *joke*.

Hazel shut her eyes against the leering portrait of Edwin Cornelius Frump and reached her arm deeper into the hole. This was crazy. The book *had* to be here.

"Aha!" Her fingers closed around the smooth, hard edge of something just within reach. But when she pulled it out, Hazel could only stare blankly at the round wooden box in her hands.

"That's not a book," Ned said unnecessarily.

Hazel held the box up to the moonlight. Then gently, slowly, she removed the lid. Ned gasped. Hazel fumbled and almost dropped the box.

Inside was a collection of jewels—a gold brooch in the shape of a flower, with sapphires for petals, a strand of pearls, diamond earrings shaped like teardrops, a delicate necklace with an emerald pendant, and a ring—a ring that held a jewel as plump and red as the juiciest raspberry.

"Whoa." Ned stared. "Is that a ruby? Hey, is this stuff real?"

Feeling as if she must be dreaming, Hazel picked up the

ring. It felt as cold and hard as ice, but in the starlight, the ruby blazed a fiery red.

Until that moment she'd never cared about jewellery. She'd thought rings were boring, and hated the time her teammates wasted before a basketball game, divesting themselves of rings, watches, earrings, necklaces. Ridiculous.

But this was different.

This was *treasure*.

· · · ·

They sat in dumbfounded silence for a long time. Eventually Ned broke the spell.

"Why didn't you tell me you'd found the jewels?" His voice squeaked in excitement. "Do you think Dad'll be mad when he finds out you discovered it early, by mistake? Hey, you know what this means? We don't need to bother finding the rest of the clues!"

Hazel tore her gaze away from the jewels to look at Ned.

"But I didn't find the treasure. I mean, not until just now. These jewels weren't here before."

"Then what did you want to show me?"

"A book."

Ned burst out laughing. "A book? You brought me here in the middle of the night to show me a book? Lucky for you we found pirate booty instead."

Hazel gave a weak smile. She felt confused; her mind was spinning in crazy directions. She didn't believe in magic. Not really. But what if the secret compartment was somehow . . . different? What if every time she opened it, she'd find something new? It might be a portal, an entrance to another dimension. Or something. Hazel didn't read science fiction, but her best friend, Alysha, did and she'd forced Hazel to listen to a lot of stuff about travelling through time and space. Then Ned would overhear and start making fun of what he called "the so-called science" and explaining why it could never happen.

No, there had to be a logical explanation. Hazel glanced around the moonlit room. Everything looked normal, or as normal as this library could look. Except . . . something wasn't quite right. She should be directly in front of the portrait of Mercy Frump.

"Of course!" Hazel smacked herself on the forehead. She and Ned were sitting *in front of the wrong bookcase.*

"Hazel? What's up?"

"We were just looking in the wrong place," Hazel muttered to herself.

"What?" Ned looked baffled. "What are you talking about?"

But Hazel was already on her belly beside the next bookcase, feeling along the baseboard for the release.

"I was so freaked out by that silly portrait, I wasn't looking where I was going," she explained. "I had you open the wrong door."

Click. The baseboard slid open, revealing the spell book exactly where she had left it hours earlier. Relief washed over Hazel; she hadn't really wanted to find a portal to another world.

"So there are *two* secret compartments?" Ned said. "What are the odds of that?"

"Around here? Anything's possible." Hazel handed him the book of spells.

"A magic book? There's no such thing as magic," Ned said dismissively. He flipped the pages idly before setting it aside. "I don't think this is part of the treasure hunt."

"I'm not sure these jewels are either," Hazel said slowly. "What if they're the lost jewels, Ned?"

Ned removed his glasses and began polishing them with the hem of his pyjama top. "You mean the ones Deirdre told us about?

The jewels everyone's been looking for, since . . . forever?"

"Yeah." Hazel turned the ruby ring over in her hands. "These look pretty old, don't you think?"

Ned nodded. "But maybe the jewels Dad hid are old. I mean, what are the odds of two sets of jewels being hidden in this castle?"

Hazel just looked at him.

"I know, I know—around here, anything's possible." Ned grinned. "Well, do we tell the others about this, or not?"

Hazel fingered the sapphire flower. If they'd really found the legendary lost jewels, all the Frumps would be excited. On the other hand, if they'd just stumbled accidentally on the jewels Charlotte and their father were using for the treasure hunt, it would spoil the fun for the adults.

"I think we wait for a bit," she said finally. "Let's keep trying to solve the clues, and at the same time, try to learn as much as we can about the lost jewels—and this treasure. I mean, we don't even know if these jewels are real. They could be fakes—what do you call 'em . . costume jewellery."

"Okay." Ned let out an enormous yawn. "And right now, I say we sleep. A box of treasure, a wacky spell book, that's a pretty good haul for one day."

They closed the secret compartments, and after some debate, agreed that Hazel would stash the jewels and magic book back in her room.

Before parting at the doorway to Oliver's room, Ned whispered, "How about we investigate the library again tomorrow, after everyone's gone? That place might be full of secret compartments."

"Shouldn't we search the walled garden for the clue first?" Hazel said.

"Fine. We'll split up—you go to the garden, and I'll go to the library. Meet me there after you find the clue."

"I thought we were against splitting up," Hazel reminded him.

"Yeah, but how much trouble can you get into in a garden?" Ned said, shaking his head.

Hazel was suddenly aware that she was exhausted. As soon as she reached her room, she wrapped the book and the jewel box in an old sweatshirt and tucked them in the storage area under her window seat. Then she crawled into bed, and fell asleep the instant her eyes closed.

Hazel was back in the library. But this time, there was no fire in the hearth; the room was empty and cold. The book of spells lay open on the table. Before Hazel could touch it, the pages began flipping as if blown by a stiff breeze. But the air was still.

Suddenly, the pages stopped. Hazel bent over the book, mesmerized by the brilliant illustration. The view was from just outside the walled garden behind the castle, and the colours were so strong and the details so lifelike, it was as if Hazel were there.

The picture wasn't quite accurate. There was no ivy covering the stone walls, and instead of a mighty oak tree in the centre of the garden, Hazel could glimpse only a young sapling through the gate. But the summer sun shone so brightly it made Hazel's eyes water. She blinked. Now the air was heavy with the scent of roses and she could hear the quiet, purposeful hum of bees. Someone laughed. Hazel looked up, but the library was still deserted. She glanced back down at the book and gasped. The library girl was in the garden, just inside the gate. Once again, her back was to Hazel, but somehow Hazel knew it was the same girl. She was gathering herbs and talking to someone in a low murmur.

But there was no one else in the garden.

An abrupt movement caught Hazel's eye. A hawk. He was perched on the branch of a flowering shrub just to the left of the girl. Was she talking to the hawk? All at once, Hazel was gripped by an overwhelming need to make the girl see her. She reached for the book, just as the hawk turned and looked past Hazel. He let out a cry, as if in warning, and suddenly Hazel knew there was someone behind her. She could hear the crunch of footsteps on gravel.

Hazel's eyes snapped open. "Whoa." She was in bed. Not in the library.

It was early morning, but there was just enough light to see that the jewels and spell book were where she'd left them under the window seat. Hazel realized she'd been holding her breath, and let it out slowly. The dream had been so vivid, so real.

Who was that girl, and why was she haunting Hazel's dreams?

It was only 7:30, but although she was tired, Hazel was too restless for sleep. She dressed wearily and wandered down to the kitchen, yawning. Uncle Seamus, Deirdre and Oliver were just putting on their jackets.

"Good morning," Uncle Seamus said. "I'm giving Deirdre and Oliver a lift to school. Are you feeling all right? You look pale."

Hazel nodded. "I'm fine. Just a bit tired."

Uncle Seamus paused in the doorway, frowning. "Perhaps I'll ask Charlotte to look in on you later today. We don't want you relapsing!"

Hazel smiled. The virus was long gone, she was sure of that. But she couldn't very well tell her uncle she was tired from prowling around his library in the middle of the night! And it was sort of nice to be fussed over . . . every once in a while.

There was no sign of Ned; he was probably fast asleep. Hazel ate breakfast alone, rinsed her cereal bowl and placed it in the dishwasher. She might as well go find the eagle and get the next clue. Luckily there were plenty of jackets by the kitchen door; she still hadn't found her windbreaker.

On her way out, Hazel stopped to scoop up a basketball from a bin of sports stuff by the kitchen door. She always felt better with a ball in her hands. And you never knew when you'd come across a patch of asphalt or stone, or some surface fit for dribbling. If she found the clue right away, maybe she could head over to the tennis court, where the Frumps had installed a basketball net last summer, and sneak in some hoops before joining Ned in the library.

Hazel started down the slope toward the lake, turning east when she reached the corner of the castle. She paused. Ahead lay the walled garden. The view was almost identical to the one in her dream—except that it was fall now, and the garden looked older. Tired. As she stood there, Hazel heard a faint sound from behind her. Footsteps on gravel.

Hazel spun around. Someone was standing at the top of the rise. It looked like a boy. He'd come by bicycle—she could see it lying at the edge of the drive. Dressed all in black, with a black helmet, the cyclist had also tied a black kerchief around the lower half of his face. Halloween was still a week away. So why was he covering his face?

The cyclist was kneeling now beside his bike. Was he a courier? He had some kind of pack with him. As Hazel watched, he pulled out a long, bulky package.

No. Not a package.

A gun.

Hazel could feel the blood in her veins turning to ice. She was frozen to the spot. She must be mistaken. It couldn't be a gun.

It was.

Every muscle in Hazel's body was screaming, telling her to do something, anything—move, run, hide, call out. Run. *Run.* But her brain was spinning out of control. Why did he have a gun? Who was this guy? How could this be happening?

Move, Hazel told herself. But she couldn't. And the questions just kept coming. Could she outrun a guy on a bike? Was it possible to dodge a bullet? How many bullets could he shoot before he'd have to stop and reload? Should she yell for help? What if Ned came?

Would he shoot her little brother?

As soon as her brain formed the thought, Hazel rejected it. No. She couldn't let that happen. And that meant she couldn't let this guy shoot her, because then she'd be helpless to protect Ned. And she *would* protect Ned.

There had to be something Hazel could do. There had to be.

The cyclist was a boy, and smaller than Hazel—could she wrestle his gun from him? No. There wasn't time. He'd pull the trigger before she could get near him.

A far-off cry rent the air. Glancing skyward, Hazel saw a hawk swooping down from one of the castle towers. The cyclist didn't notice. He had raised his gun. He was taking aim. He was going to shoot her.

A voice sounded in Hazel's head. *Shoot first. Shoot the ball!*

The voice was crazy. A basketball against a gun? But it might buy her some time. Hazel threw the ball as hard as she could. It was a playoff-style, take-no-prisoners pass and it hurtled through the air faster than any pass she'd ever thrown.

The ball slammed into the cyclist; he tripped and fell, dropping the gun. For a split second, Hazel paused. Could she get to the gun before he did? Then the cyclist got to his knees and Hazel realized there was no way, no chance, he was only seconds away from picking up that gun and now she had nothing, no weapon, and all she could do was turn and run.

The garden wasn't that far, and its walls were eight feet high and built of thick stone. Maybe, just maybe, if she ran faster than she ever had before—but then the hawk cried out again, and something thudded to the ground behind her, just missing her heels. Hazel redoubled her efforts to reach the garden, pumping her legs furiously. Her chest felt as if it was being squeezed; she was gulping for air. But the garden gate was just ahead.

She almost made it.

Another projectile slammed into the stone wall just ahead of her. Hazel stumbled and went sprawling in the dirt. She closed her eyes instinctively as she fell, but not before noticing a bright blue stain spreading across the garden wall.

Paint. Blue paint.

He was shooting a paintball gun.

Hazel gasped. Now she knew what people meant when they said they didn't know whether to laugh or cry.

This was a million times better than a real gun firing real bullets. But paintballs were still dangerous, and it occurred to Hazel that jeans and a light jacket weren't exactly what you'd call protective gear.

In that instant, a tiny blue pellet exploded against her leg.

"Ow! Hey, stop that, you idiot!" Hazel's voice shook with fury. "You could take someone's eye out with that!"

She rose to her feet unsteadily, one arm shielding her face, in case he fired again. But now that he'd actually hit her, the boy seemed to be in shock, staring at the gun in his hands. His kerchief had slipped down around his neck, but his bike helmet had come loose, tilting forward so that it obscured his face. Hazel couldn't tell if he'd heard her.

"What's the matter with you?" She started limping toward him, anger pumping through her veins. "That wasn't funny!"

Even the hawk seemed to feel the crisis had passed. He gave one last cry as he wheeled overhead and then took off over the lake, toward the Martello tower.

The cyclist shook his head and snapped back to life. Stuffing the gun back in his pack, he yanked his bike off the ground and snarled, "It wasn't supposed to be funny."

Hazel stopped in her tracks. She knew that voice. It reeked of self-pity and anger.

"I hate you, Hazel Frump. I HATE you!" The boy pushed the helmet back off his face and glared at her.

"Kenny? Kenny Pritchard?"

Kenny didn't answer. Hazel watched as he turned the bike around. She made no move to follow him. But she could hear him sobbing angrily as he cycled slowly down the drive.

Suddenly, Hazel wasn't in the mood for clues or a treasure hunt. Still favouring her left leg, she climbed the steps to the veranda and let herself into the kitchen.

When Ned finally came down for breakfast, he found Hazel slumped in one of the armchairs, staring at the embers in the fireplace without seeing them. She didn't look up. She was still trying to decide whether to say anything about Kenny. On the one hand, maybe she'd done enough to Kenny already. On the other hand, wouldn't the world seem like a safer place if a grown-up knew the kid had flipped out and started riding around the island firing paintballs at people?

"Uh . . . Hazel? Why do you have paint on your jeans?"

The sound of her brother's voice was all it took to make up Hazel's mind. It was one thing for Kenny to come after her. But what if it had been Ned? She sat up straighter.

"We have to call Uncle Seamus," she said, "right now."

Ned's eyes were wide as he watched Hazel dial, and they grew wider as he listened to her tell Uncle Seamus what had happened. Luckily, Uncle Seamus didn't interrupt. Just talking about it made Hazel feel angry and guilty and afraid all over again. The only detail she left out was the hawk; it was too eerily reminiscent of her dream. If Hazel were asked to compile a list of things that grownups had difficulty with, prophetic dreams and inexplicable animal behaviour would be right up there.

After she'd hung up, Ned asked what Uncle Seamus had said.

"He's sending Charlotte over as soon as he can reach her, just to make sure I'm okay. But I am okay, really. And he's coming home early, too. But first he's going to the Pritchards', to have a talk with Kenny's mum."

Ned hadn't eaten breakfast yet, she realized. At her urging, he wolfed down a bowl of cereal. But as soon as he finished, Ned grabbed her hand and began pulling Hazel toward the door. "Come on, you need a distraction. Let's go find that clue."

Hazel was surprised to realize she felt a little nervous being outside. She kept glancing over her shoulder, thinking she could hear the sound of bike tires. The sky was now a brilliant blue and the sun had turned the lake into a sapphire so dazzling her eyes hurt to look at it. A fresh breeze rustled through the few dry leaves that still clung to the trees and made the reeds at the water's edge dance. Across the channel, the old Martello tower stood watch over the treacherous currents.

"It seems like just yesterday that we used the stinkbombs to trap Clive Pritchard there, and you swam across . . . I bet you he wishes he could be outside in the sun right now," Ned said.

Hazel managed a smile and squeezed his hand. He was trying to cheer her up, she knew. But having someone aim a gun at you—even a fake one—wasn't all that easy to shake off.

The old garden was completely enclosed by meandering walls of limestone. Over time, creeping vines and sprays of climbing roses had hidden most of the stone, until the garden appeared to be surrounded by a living wall. To Hazel the garden was beautiful, but wistful. Though Ned was at her side, she felt lonely.

The iron gate creaked as it swung slowly closed behind them. Even *it* sounded sad, Hazel reflected.

Ned led the way down a narrow path of gravel that was flanked by slender trees that stretched their delicate, twisting arms until they met, high above the children's heads. The path ended at a stone fountain, ringed with some kind of herb. Other alleys branched off to the left and right. Hazel and Ned took the left and soon found themselves surrounded by yew trees clipped into curious shapes. Just beyond the yews, an entire section of the garden had been filled by rose bushes. There were no blooms, but Hazel recognized the arching sprays of the climbing roses, and the stiff, shorter stems of the hybrid teas.

And there, just between the yews and the roses, stood a statue of an eagle.

He was an oddly cheery-looking bird. Hazel had always thought of eagles as imperious, haughty, yet some stone carver had managed to make this eagle look like he had just discovered it was his birthday. But there was no clue on the statue.

"It's been awfully windy the last few days," Ned pointed out. "Maybe the clue blew away?"

They got down on hands and knees and began to search the nearby rose bushes, wincing as the brambles scratched their skin.

"There it is!"

Hazel followed Ned's pointing finger and saw a yellow envelope, hanging by a piece of tape from a thorny-looking branch. But before she could grab it, a mournful creak sounded behind them.

Someone had opened the iron gate.

CHAPTER EIGHT

Hazel and Ned crouched beside the rose bush. Hazel's pulse was racing. Should they confront the intruder? Should they hide? It couldn't be Kenny, could it? Even he wouldn't be crazy enough to come back. The impulse to flee was strong; Hazel could feel the muscles in her leg twitching.

"Ned? Hazel? It's only me. Where'd you go?"

It was Charlotte. With a sigh of relief, Ned got to his feet. Hazel found she was shaking slightly and unable to speak.

Ned shot a worried glance at her before hollering, "We're over here—in the roses." Ned ran down the gravel path in the direction of Charlotte's voice, waving his arms and hollering, "Over here!"

Hazel slowly stood up and took several deep, steadying breaths. Then she reached into the brambles and plucked the clue from its thorny prison, jamming it into her pocket before turning to see Charlotte and Ned rounding the corner toward her.

"Hey, Charlotte." Hazel was pleased to hear how steady her own voice sounded. "Thanks for coming over."

Wordlessly, Charlotte enveloped her in a giant hug. Hazel was too taken aback at first to return the hug.

"I'm okay, really," she told her cousin. "It was just paint—see?"

Charlotte held Hazel by the shoulders and examined the blue splotch on her jeans. "You'll probably have a nasty bruise by the end of the day. What was that boy thinking?"

Hazel shrugged and tried to look unbothered, but Ned's eyes were dark.

"Revenge!" he said in a sombre voice. "Kenny was thinking of revenge."

Charlotte sighed. Looping an arm around each of their shoulders, she led the way out of the garden.

Over steaming mugs of hot chocolate, Charlotte told them that Uncle Seamus had already spoken with Kenny's mother and with the local constable, who had announced that he was running out of patience with the Pritchards. Kenny's mother had organized a meeting that afternoon with Uncle Seamus and the constable, where Kenny would write a formal apology to Hazel and agree to whatever community service the adults thought could "set him straight."

Hazel felt a burst of relief. It was followed almost immediately by guilt.

"Kenny scared me and what he did was really wrong, but . . . I did put his dad in jail," she began, but Charlotte cut her off.

"The *police* put his father in jail."

"Well, Kenny sure blames me for messing up his life."

Charlotte sighed. "Kenny's life was, as you so eloquently put it, 'messed up' long before you came along. Your compassion does you credit, but Kenny doesn't need people making excuses for him or looking the other way when he misbehaves."

"You said the meeting this afternoon was his mother's idea?" Ned asked.

Charlotte nodded. "I think the arrest of the Pritchards was a wake-up call for his mum. After years of letting Kenny and his dad get away with anything, she's finally trying to do what's right. She's worried that if he doesn't start taking responsibility for his actions, he'll end up like his dad."

"So what do we do now?" Ned asked.

"Let's let your uncle and the police sort things out and you two just take it easy." Charlotte gave Hazel a searching look. "You look like you could use some peace and quiet. Now, I promised Seamus I'd stick around until he gets home. Do you kids want to hang out with me or would you rather be on your own? Should I fix you a snack? I've got a new recipe for muffins I'd like to try."

At the word *muffins* Hazel's mouth began to water, but Ned grabbed her arm.

"We actually have some homework to do—at least, Hazel does. And I'm helping. Would it be okay if we worked in the library while you bake?"

Charlotte's smile was quizzical but she nodded, and promised to have muffins ready in time for afternoon tea. On the way to the library, Hazel handed Ned the clue.

"You did get it, after all!" Ned slapped Hazel on the back. "I figured we'd have to sneak out again later."

They paused by one of the stained glass windows and Ned unfolded the paper. Together they read:

Follow the narrow path that winds;
You do not need a clew.
Seek me underneath the stone,
Near an abandoned pew.

"Hey, look: *clue* is spelled wrong." Ned looked pleased at spotting the error.

But Hazel wondered. "I don't think that's the kind of mistake Dad or Charlotte would make." She glanced down the hall, toward the library door. "I wish this place followed the Dewey Decimal system. Or any system! We need a dictionary."

"We could go back to the kitchen and look it up in that big dictionary, but Charlotte's there." Ned snapped his fingers. "Oliver's room has a dictionary—and we might need his computer too. C'mon."

Finding Oliver's dictionary meant minutes of pawing through piles of discarded clothing.

"Nothing's actually dirty," Ned said, watching Hazel pinch her nose and nudge a heap of socks and T-shirts with the toe of her sneaker. "It's just clirty. You know—a cross between clean and dirty! You don't put 'em in the hamper 'cause you could wear them again. If you had to."

"Charming." Hazel's toe connected with something solid. "Hang on, I think this is it."

The dictionary yielded the information that a clew was something used in sailing or to suspend a hammock. But further on it said: "the ball of yarn or thread used by Theseus to find his way out of the labyrinth."

"Of course—I remember the story now," Ned said excitedly. "Theseus and the Minotaur, right? We learned this in school. He has to kill a monster, this Minotaur, and he uses thread to find his way out of a maze. Excellent! What kind of monster do you think we'll face?"

"Calm down, the clues are supposed to be 'simple, safe and fun'—remember?" Hazel gave a grim laugh. "I might get trapped in a dungeon or shot at by a crazy boy with a paintball gun, but I draw the line at monsters."

Ned's face fell. "Rats. For a second I thought maybe Uncle Seamus had some kind of mutant snake or giant reptile living in the cellar. What's the point of raising our hopes with all this 'clew' talk if there's no monster? It's mean."

"Oh, Ned. You're disappointed because there isn't an actual Minotaur? Look, it does say we have to follow a winding path, so I think the clew part is Dad's way of saying we're looking for a maze."

"Okay—what maze?"

There was silence for a few minutes. Hazel wondered whether Charlotte would have had time to make the muffins yet. She glanced at her watch. Probably not.

"I give up. Let's just go to your room and look at the jewels some more," Ned said.

"Or we could go back to the library," Hazel said slowly.

"Why?"

"I know this may sound strange, but I think the library's important somehow." Hazel hesitated. She hadn't confided in Ned about her dreams yet. But in the past, he had been the one person who took her nightmares seriously.

Drawing in a deep breath, Hazel quickly described her dreams about the girl in the library and the garden. She even told him about the hawk. Ned listened without interrupting, his face thoughtful. When she had finished, he sat in silence for a few minutes, before peppering her with questions.

"So, who do you think the girl is? And what makes you think it's the library that's so important—wasn't she in the garden the second time? And what's with the hawk?"

Hazel pulled at her hair and tried not to groan.

"I don't know who the girl is, but she seems to belong with the castle, and she's definitely from a long time ago, because her clothes are really old-fashioned." Hazel paused and Ned nodded in a "go on" kind of way.

"And I'm not sure exactly why I feel the library's important but we did find the jewels and the weird spell book there," Hazel said. "Why couldn't it be hiding something else? I know we found two things already, but in fables and fairy tales there's always one more: three wishes, three guesses, three ghosts for Ebenezer Scrooge . . ."

"That's just crazy talk." Ned folded his arms across his chest.

Hazel had to admit that it sounded odd, but she pressed on. "I think the hawk's the crazy part. I have this feeling I've seen that bird before," she said. "Maybe it has something to do with the storm, when I was lost in the woods. But I can't remember, no matter how hard I try. It's driving me nuts."

Ned put his glasses back on and studied his sister. "You're not nuts."

"Thanks." Hazel threw him a grateful smile.

"You *sound* nuts, but that's normal for you."

"Gee, thanks."

"There are things science can't explain," Ned continued, ignoring Hazel's glare. "Yet. I'm not talking about your wacky good-things-come-in-threes idea. That's just silly. But we already know somebody has used the library to hide stuff, so you're right: it makes sense to check for more. And we already know that your dreams are different from most people's dreams, so even though we don't know what they mean yet, we won't ignore them."

Hazel nodded. "But I don't feel like just waiting around for the next dream. I want to do something, figure out how everything is connected. *If* it's connected."

"We should bring in some extra help," Ned said. "We need the cousins on our team—Oliver and Deirdre for starters, and then Matt and Mark when they come back from university. Except it's against the rule."

"It's a dumb rule. You'd think Dad would have realized by now that secrets aren't the way to go." But Hazel could feel the stirrings of an idea. "Wait. That first note from Dad and Charlotte only said we couldn't consult uncles or cousins."

"Yeah, but who else is there around here?"

"Right." Hazel sighed. "Who says it has to be someone from around here, anyway? We could call Frankie!"

Frankie was their neighbour back home. She lived across the hall from them, in the warehouse Colin Frump had converted into lofts. Frankie was a scatterbrain, but devoted to Hazel and Ned. Plus, she was the sort of scatterbrain who knew all sorts of surprising things and people. Ned made straight for the phone.

"Oh, it's so good to hear your voice!" Frankie said. "I miss you guys so much when you're away at school."

"We miss you too," Ned replied. "But we're not actually *at* school."

Hazel had picked up the extension, but even with both of them on the phone it took forever to fill Frankie in on everything that had happened, particularly since she kept interrupting to complain about their father and his penchant for secrecy. By the time Hazel got to the discovery of the jewels, Frankie had to go.

"But I'm dying to see these jewels. You've got your digital camera, don't you, Ned? Can you send me a picture?"

"Yes," Ned said. "But we're not even sure the jewels are real, Frankie."

"Perhaps I can help with that. I may not be able to tell from just a photo, but I do know some people who might. I'll post the images on Sketchbook and let you know what I find out, okay? Bye!"

Frankie had recently joined an artists' social networking site on the Internet. She complained that it distracted her from painting, but she seemed to be addicted, and spent an enormous amount of time e-mailing friends all over the world.

Hazel glanced at the grandfather clock beside the window. Charlotte would be summoning them soon for that snack. They'd better divvy up the tasks. Ned took care of the technical side of things, hurrying to Hazel's room to photograph the jewels and then back to download the file onto Oliver's computer, while Hazel wrote a lengthy e-mail that would bring Frankie up to date. Ned attached his photo file to Hazel's e-mail and had just hit Send when they heard Charlotte ringing the kitchen bell.

"Good timing," Hazel said, as they scurried down the hall.

"Yup." With his fingers, Ned began ticking off a list: "Now all we have left to do is search the library for any other secret compartments, find the rest of the clues, and solve the treasure hunt . . ."

". . . and do my history homework," Hazel finished on a resigned note.

"Your homework?"

"Yes. *Something* obviously happened here long ago. And since I'm supposed to be finding out what life was like back in the 1800s anyway, we might as well start there."

But the research would have to wait. The rest of the day was taken up by modern-day Frumps and their efforts to reassure Hazel and Ned that nothing like Kenny's paintball attack would ever happen again at Land's End. There were muffins and more hugs with Charlotte, followed by the appearance of Uncle Seamus, even more hugs, and a long talk about how seriously Kenny's mother was taking the incident.

When Deirdre and Oliver returned home, they told the family the story had spread throughout the school like a virus, mutating slightly as it moved from student to student. At least Hazel didn't have to retell everything. All she had to do was reassure her cousins that she wasn't actually blinded in one eye, or brain-damaged, and that Kenny had not tried to set fire to the castle before leaving.

"I knew that part couldn't be true," Oliver said, in a voice that suggested otherwise.

Charlotte couldn't stay for dinner; she wanted to check on

how Kenny Pritchard's mother was coping at the end of a long day. Ned took advantage of her absence to violate the treasure hunt rule about consulting cousins or uncles. Hazel admired the brazen way he paused between mouthfuls to ask:

"So, are there any mazes or labyrinths around here?"

The great thing about this family, Hazel decided, was that his question struck no one at the table as odd.

"There's a corn maze at Mimi Deacon's farm, down the road. Do you guys want to go?" Oliver asked.

Ned leaned forward. "That depends. What's a corn maze?"

"You know, the farmer plants a field of corn, then mows a twisty path with lots of dead ends, and charges people to go through it. The Deacons have maze nights too, where they give you flashlights and send you out to get lost. I don't like those as much. It's all dark and spooky, 'cause the wind rustles the corn and you can't figure out how to escape."

Ned's eyes met Hazel's and she gave a tiny shrug.

"Yeah, maybe we should check it out sometime," Ned said casually. "But not at night. It would be too hard to see."

"That's sort of the point," Deirdre said.

"Right. I meant, uh, too spooky. Cold, too." Ned looked around the table. "Anyone know any other mazes?"

But nobody did.

After dinner, Uncle Seamus said he was heading to his study to work, and Hazel said she and Ned might just go read in the library. To her chagrin, Deirdre and Oliver said they'd come along.

The library was chilly, and Deirdre lit a fire. As she and Oliver bickered comfortably over which of them should get the softest armchair, Ned and Hazel wandered around the room, surreptitiously tapping on baseboards and knocking on wooden carvings while they pretended to look for something to read.

Eventually, of course, Deirdre noticed.

"What's with all the noise?" she said. "Some of us are trying to read!" And she pointed to a trio of wooden plaques mounted high on the wall, each inscribed with a different word in Latin: SAPIENTIA, DOCTRINA, SILENTIUM.

"I don't get it," Hazel said.

"Wisdom, knowledge, silence," Deirdre intoned solemnly. Then she ruined the effect by giggling. "Of course, you don't have to be silent; it's not like this is a real library. But if you could keep it down?"

Oliver looked up from his book. "If you guys are trying to get a bookcase to slide open and reveal a secret passageway, you can forget it. Mark and I already tried that one summer, when it rained for eighteen days straight."

"Oh." Ned gave a sheepish grin. "Okay then."

Hazel decided she might as well look for something to read. But she was soon distracted. In one of the darkest recesses of the library, she came across several folders stuffed with yellowing papers—drawings, old postcards, sketches.

"What a jumble," Hazel said. A postcard dated 1974 was somehow stuck to the envelope of a letter from 1942 and a menu from a diner in 1964.

"Hazel," Ned hissed. "Come here, you need to see this."

"Coming." She started to replace the folder, but a piece of paper escaped, fluttering to the floor. It was an old, faded sketch of someone in a garden. Hazel bent to pick it up, and stared.

It was the girl from the dream.

And sitting on her shoulder was a hawk.

CHAPTER NINE

So the girl in her dreams was real. Hazel's stomach did flip-flops. How could she dream about someone she'd never met—someone she'd never even seen?

Hazel opened the folder again, shuffling through the papers. There had to be something else about the girl, some clue to her identity. A faded newspaper clipping caught Hazel's eye. The headline read: "Local Taxidermist Travels to London."

Edwin Frump, of Île du Loup, has journeyed to England to hone his taxidermy skills with learned practitioners such as Peter Spicer and Thomas Gunn. The Frump family plans to open a natural history museum upon his return.

Huh. Hazel wondered if that had ever happened. Judging by the hallway of dead, dancing animals upstairs, she guessed not. Creepy Edwin. It figured he'd be the one who liked to work with dead things.

"Hazel, you need to see this!" Ned tugged at her elbow. "I found this in a box of old sketches—it's a map of Land's End."

Hazel gently smoothed the brittle paper. The drawing was

lovely—an artist's rendering of the castle and grounds from long ago.

She could see all the familiar landmarks: the castle itself, the walled garden, the orchard, the vegetable garden, and the nearby island with the Martello tower. But the drawing also showed flower beds, stables and an apiary where now there stood a tennis court and a towering forest of pine trees. Ned tapped the corner of the sketch, where a tiny building, like a miniature church, stood at the end of a winding path. The ink was faded but she thought she could make out the word *chapel*.

"The clue is supposed to be near an abandoned pew, right?" Ned said.

Hazel nodded.

"What have you got there?" Ned asked.

"A bunch of weird stuff. It turns out Edwin was our taxidermist." Hazel handed him the clipping. "But Ned—this sketch? It's the girl. The one I dreamed about."

Ned showed more interest in the clipping than the sketch. Hazel wondered if he even believed that it was the same girl, but then Ned said, "There are probably other pictures of her around here, and you must have seen one. Your conscious mind doesn't remember seeing it, but deep down you do, and you put her in your dream. I told you there was probably a simple, scientific explanation."

Hazel couldn't have said why, but Ned's reasoning irritated her. Could it really be that simple?

"Hey, Oliver, can we use your computer?" Ned asked.

"Sure, but you better act fast." Oliver looked at the clock. "Dad's gonna show up any minute to remind us it's bedtime."

Hazel wanted to stay and look through the other folders, but Ned was pushing her out the door.

"What's the rush?"

83

"I want to try something on Google. We need to find out what a chapel and a maze have to do with each other."

Typing the word *labyrinth* into the search engine turned up movies, books and rock groups, not to mention loads of online video games that required players to find their way out of mazes. But when Hazel changed the parameters of the search, typing the words *labyrinth* and *church*, the pieces fell into place.

"Most scholars today agree a maze and a labyrinth are not the same thing," Hazel read aloud, her voice quickening in excitement. "A maze is a puzzle, with multiple paths branching off in all directions, and many dead ends. It is designed to trick and confuse. A labyrinth has one path only, and is walked by those on a spiritual journey. Many different religions all over the world use the labyrinth for contemplation."

Hazel glanced at Ned. "Did you know a maze and a labyrinth aren't the same thing?"

"Nope." Ned pointed to several diagrams on the screen. "This is weird. Some of these labyrinths are really simple—follow the path and you get to the centre in seconds. But check out that one. It makes you wander all over the place, like it's forcing you to slow down and take forever to get there."

"Maybe that's the point," Hazel said. "If you just cut to the centre it's not much of a journey, is it?"

She scrolled down the page. "That one's at the Chartres Cathedral in France. And oh, oh look, it says this type of labyrinth is sometimes called a pavement labyrinth because it's laid into the stones of the floor!"

Ned pulled out the clue again and read aloud: "'Follow the narrow path that winds. . . Seek me *underneath the stone*'! That has to be it! There must be a labyrinth in that chapel!"

They found it next to impossible to sleep that night. They were so close to discovering the next clue. And every time Hazel started to drift off, strange images floated into her mind—the girl with the hawk, holding the giant ruby ring . . . Edwin holding the paw of a dancing fox . . .

Hazel was relieved when morning came. It seemed odd to her that there was no sign of Uncle Seamus, Deirdre or Oliver in the kitchen at 7:00, but Ned was already there and dressed, finishing a bowl of cold cereal. Hazel made toast, but the incessant drumming of Ned's fingers on the table convinced her to take it along as they searched for the clue.

In the years since the diagram was drawn, thick woods had sprung up on the southeastern side of the castle. But it didn't take long before Hazel and Ned were standing in a clearing staring at a tumbledown structure that they knew at once had been a place for prayer. Ivy and moss had crept over the crumbling walls of fieldstone, turning everything green. The chapel almost seemed to be alive. But instead of growing, it was decaying. It was strangely beautiful. Ned had brought his digital camera along, and he took it out now to snap a few pictures.

"I'm glad all the snow and ice are gone," he observed.

"That was just a freak storm," Hazel said absently. "It's . . . what, October twenty-fifth? We don't often get snow before Halloween."

The wooden door squeaked on its hinges and yielded reluctantly to her push. She entered first, with Ned close on her heels. It took a moment for their eyes to adjust to the gloom, but it wasn't as dark as Hazel had expected—dappled sunlight found its way in through two narrow windows and a gaping hole in the roof. They could see two rows of simple wooden pews, divided by a narrow aisle.

"Look!" Ned pointed to the area in front of the pews. A faded carpet, mud-stained and covered in leaves, concealed much of the floor. But one corner of the rug had flipped back to reveal the stone tiles underneath. Something was drawn on the stone.

Within seconds, they had rolled up the carpet and exposed the floor. Hazel exhaled slowly. There it was: a pavement labyrinth. Much smaller and not as fancy as the one in the Chartres Cathedral, but still pretty cool.

"I guess we start walking the labyrinth." And with an air of solemnity, Hazel stepped onto the first tile. But before she could take another step, Ned sprang forward, cutting across the looping paths to the rosette in the centre of the labyrinth.

One of the stones in the rosette was slightly out of place, sitting higher than the others. He pried it up with his fingers, revealing an orange envelope underneath.

"Got it!" he yelled.

Hazel rolled her eyes. So much for following the path of enlightenment.

"Okay, let's put the carpet back and get out of here," she said.

Ned thrust the orange envelope into her hands. "You read. I'll lead the way back through the woods. The last time you tried to take a shortcut through a forest it didn't work out so well."

"Funny. Okay, here goes:"

Across from me
There is a key
(No lock),
A court without a jury.

Behind my door
There is a store
(A clock),
Troops marching in a hurry.

Ned let out a low whistle. "These clues just get weirder and weirder. I hope Dad's almost done."

On their way back to the castle, they paused at the tennis court. Ned scooped up a basketball that was lying by the fence.

"Oh, Mr. Spalding," he said. "Can't you please help us decipher the latest clue?"

Hazel laughed. Ned tossed the ball toward her but as she moved automatically to catch it, a thought struck Hazel with such force that she halted abruptly. The ball bounced off her head and rolled to a stop at Ned's feet.

"Gee, Hazel, I'm sorry. Are you okay?"

Hazel blinked. "I'm more than okay. I've got it—at least, I've solved the first half of the clue."

"What are you talking about?"

Hazel flung out an arm dramatically. "What is this place, Ned?"

"Uh, it's a tennis court. With a basketball net at one end. Are you sure that ball didn't hit you too hard?"

"It's a *court*." Hazel waved the clue in his face. "And just down the road in Ville St-Pierre, what kind of court is there?"

"Oh. A basketball court! Where we played last summer, against Kenny Pritchard and Hank Packham and that Billy guy." Ned smacked his forehead. "I get it. That's the kind of court where there's no jury!"

"And a basketball court doesn't have a lock but it does have a *key*." She gestured toward the area under the basket, where she hoped someday Uncle Seamus would mark out a proper key with painted lines.

"Nice." Ned reached up to slap palms. "Now all we have to do is figure out the last verse, and we're set!"

"Set for what?" Oliver asked.

Hazel and Ned turned to see Deirdre following him onto the tennis court.

"What are you guys doing home?" Ned asked. "I thought you'd left for school already."

"It's a holiday." Oliver frowned. "Don't you remember me complaining about having to go back to school on Thursday when we'd have Friday off while they fumigate the building?"

"Oh yeah, sorry."

"So Oliver and I decided we'd take you to that corn maze we were telling you about. It's actually at my best friend's farm," Deirdre said. "Oliver's nervous about getting lost in there, so I've arranged for her to go through it with us. And she's asked us to stay for lunch."

"Oh, but . . ." Hazel began, and then stopped. She had been going to say they didn't need to see the corn maze anymore; they'd already found the clue. But Deirdre and Oliver had gone to some trouble to arrange the outing.

"Sounds great," Ned said.

"It does," Hazel agreed. "But do you mind if I stick around here to work on that homework assignment? We'll be heading back to school in a week or so and I still have a lot of work to do."

Privately, Hazel admitted to herself that although she would work on the history assignment, she was truly hoping to learn more about the girl in the sketch. But Deirdre and Oliver just shrugged, accepting her excuse. Only Ned looked concerned.

"Are you sure you'll be okay on your own?"

"Actually, she won't be on her own," Deirdre said. "Dad's working from home today—he's in his study."

Hazel watched from the veranda as Ned and their cousins cycled down the long, tree-lined drive. Discordant honking filled the air as a large, wobbly V of Canada geese flew past, one or two stragglers hurrying to catch up. The sun was shining through the trees, but Hazel could suddenly feel November hovering; the moist air held a hint of the cold that lay in wait. Along the drive, enormous maple trees still smouldered

red, and in the fields, the goldenrod still burned. But already the grass had disappeared beneath a flame-coloured carpet of fallen leaves and the spice of woodsmoke flavoured the air.

"Time to get to work." Turning her back on autumn, Hazel went in search of the nineteenth century, and the girl.

Today the library seemed a welcoming place. Sunlight streamed through the stained glass dome overhead, warming the room and illuminating the dust particles that danced in the air. The room seemed less musty than usual, and there was even a hint of a breeze; someone had left one of the narrow, Gothic windows slightly ajar.

Hazel retrieved the folder with the sketch of the girl, and carried several other folders stuffed with miscellaneous papers over to one of the long library tables. It was as if someone had gathered armfuls of stray papers from around the castle in a sudden burst of tidying, and tucked them away to be sorted later. Only later had never come.

Hazel ignored the recipes, bookmarks and doodles—along with most of the postcards and letters. Someday, perhaps, she'd go through them to see if there was anything her dad had contributed when he was growing up at Land's End. But for now, she really just wanted to learn more about the girl, the hawk or the legendary lost jewels.

"What's this?" A torn bit of newspaper caught Hazel's eye. Without the rest of the paper, she had no way of knowing the date it was published, but the name of that murdered politician leaped off the page: Thomas D'Arcy McGee.

Montreal businessman James Pritchard has denied claims his family has ties to the Fenian brotherhood. Accused of privately backing Patrick Whelan, the Fenian hanged for the murder of Thomas D'Arcy McGee, Mr. Pritchard said he had only a passing acquaintance with the man, and never supplied him with sums of money for the Irish cause.

Pritchard? Like Kenny and his uncle? Hazel shook her head. Pritchard was a pretty common name. It had to be a coincidence.

There was nothing else in that folder about the Fenians or Thomas D'Arcy McGee. But the next folder made Hazel sit up straighter. Sandwiched between someone's project on the life cycle of a tree and a bunch of children's drawings were two more sketches of the girl.

The first drawing showed her in the garden, gathering herbs. There was a blurred signature at the bottom, very faint, but it looked as if the first name started with the letter *K*. The second drawing showed the girl dressed up as if for a party, and she was wearing a jewelled pin in the shape of a flower. Hazel didn't need to check the jewels in her room to know that it was the sapphire pin.

For a few moments she sat there and stared at the drawing, her mind racing with questions. Was this proof that the jewels she and Ned had found were the lost jewels, after all? Hazel tore through the rest of the folders, but there was nothing else about the girl, the hawk or the treasure.

• • • •

Hazel found it impossible to work on her history assignment now. Restless, she wandered around the room, stretching stiff muscles, thinking. She walked up to the portrait of Edwin Cornelius Frump and peered at the old man. For the first time she noticed the portrait included a mouse, cowering in the corner. Strange.

"You, sir, do not look like a nice man." She paused. "I hope you stayed in England."

She turned on her heel and walked away. Ned would think she was nuts, talking to a painting. She paused in front of the much cheerier portrait of Mercy Frump.

"Okay, I need to know who that girl was. I'm not going to ask Creepy Edwin over there. But you look nice. You'd tell me, if you could. Right?"

Hazel smiled. Ned really would think she was crazy. Hazel studied the painting. There was something oddly familiar about the old woman, and the graceful way she held herself. In the portrait, Mercy was sewing by the light of an open window. Hazel peered at the background. Something was in the tree just outside that window, a sort of brown blur, obscured by leaves.

A hawk.

Hazel gasped. Her eyes moved back and forth between the hawk and the woman. It was suddenly so clear: Mercy Frump was the girl from her dreams! She felt a rush of shame for not having recognized it sooner, but in the dreams and in the sketches, Mercy seemed only a few years older than Hazel. Here, her hair was the soft grey of a dove and her skin was lined.

Hazel's reverie was interrupted by the small but insistent sound of scratching. It was coming from behind her. She turned slowly, but saw nothing. Until a sudden movement caught her eye, and she realized she was no longer alone in the room.

CHAPTER TEN

The hawk perched on the sill of the open window. His majestic head swivelled, and he fixed Hazel with his golden eye. She could hardly breathe. She felt as if he was waiting for her to do something. To speak?

"Uh . . . hello?" Hazel croaked. But the hawk did nothing. He didn't even blink.

Hazel could feel a faint flush spreading across her face. Talking to portraits was one thing—but now she was addressing a wild bird! Did she really expect him to answer? To talk?

Actually, Hazel admitted silently, she kind of did.

"You know, it's not normal for a wild bird to just . . . walk into someone's house," Hazel said. "Are you hurt or sick or something?"

The hawk took a tiny step forward, and the thought flashed into Hazel's mind that perhaps he really was sick. Something seemed to be wrong with his right wing—an injury? Maybe he'd been attacked by a rabid animal and now he had rabies. Could birds get rabies? People could catch rabies from infected animals, Hazel knew that much.

She took a step backward.

The hawk stared at her before slowly turning his head until he was staring at a point high on the upper wall, above the cat-walk that encircled the room. Hazel followed his gaze. She saw nothing out of the ordinary. Just shelves of dusty books, and above them, one of the plaques Deirdre had pointed out the other day, the one inscribed with the Latin word for silence: *silentium*.

There was no logical reason why she should feel like the hawk wanted her to go up there. Hazel could see the plaque just fine from down here. She hated heights. Not that a hawk would understand that.

Taking a deep breath, Hazel moved toward the stairs.

The catwalk was perhaps six feet wide, and its wooden floor felt solid. More of a balcony, really, Hazel told herself. Nothing creaked as she inched toward the Latin sign. Still, Hazel kept close to the bookcases, and as far as possible from the elegant, wrought-iron railing over which she could see the lower level.

This would never pass a modern building safety inspection, she thought, trying not to look at the great gaps between the railings. You could drive a truck through them. It would be awfully easy for a person to slip through . . .

She was standing underneath the SILENTIUM plaque now. Hazel blinked. What was she doing up here, anyway? Clearly, her imagination had carried her away. She should go find Uncle Seamus and tell him there was a crazy, rabid bird in the library, and people around here shouldn't leave windows open. Except—the bird was gone.

Feeling incredibly foolish, Hazel was about to retrace her steps, when the background of the Edwin Frump portrait caught her eye. He had been painted in this very room. But viewed from this angle, something about the library in the painting was different.

"Oh! It's the words! The words are wrong!"

Creepy Edwin had obviously posed for his portrait roughly where Hazel was standing now. She turned around. The plaque above her head read SILENTIUM: silence. But in the painting it read VERITAS.

"So who changed the plaque?" Hazel said. "And why change *truth* into *silence?*"

There was only one thing to do. Hazel grasped the sides of one of the tall, rolling ladders that were hooked onto the railing high on the wall and pulled until it lined up alongside the plaque. Climbing the ladder took all her willpower. The balcony had been bad enough. Somehow the ladder, even though it was attached to a railing, seemed awfully precarious.

Hazel's palms were sweating by the time she reached the plaque. Refusing to look down, she concentrated instead on the large brass letters mounted on polished wood. She forced the trembling fingers of one hand to let go of the ladder and rapped the wall with her knuckles. It didn't sound—wait—that *did* sound hollow! Hazel tugged at the edges of the plaque. It was hinged, like the secret compartment in the baseboard, turning the plaque into a cupboard door. But the hinges were stiff and it took a few moments before the plaque creaked open.

Hazel thrust her hand inside the hollowed-out space in the stone wall behind. Maybe there would be more treasure. Perhaps a sword with a jewelled hilt? Or a chest filled with gold coins?

No: a book.

Hazel groaned. The small, cloth-bound volume was the only thing hidden behind the plaque.

"All this for another book." Hazel closed the secret compartment again and picked her way cautiously down the ladder, and then the spiral staircase.

Safely back on the main floor of the library, Hazel sank into one of the armchairs by the empty fireplace. She blew some of the dust from the book's cover, but there was no title.

Flipping through the first few pages, Hazel saw that like the book of spells, this was written by hand. But in this book, each entry was marked by a date—no year, just the day and month. A diary, then, or a journal? Which ancestor had kept the diary? Whoever it was, he or she hadn't signed a name.

She curled up in the chair and began to read.

The diary had belonged to a young man and was clearly one of a series of journals he'd kept. This one picked up shortly after his arrival at Land's End from Montreal, and the first few entries went on at length about the food and the furnishings of his room, the tranquility of the castle grounds and the recently planted gardens.

Hazel yawned. So far, the only truly interesting things were his little sketches. Every once in a while his entries would be interrupted by a pencil drawing of a bird or a plant. Once there was even a tiny self-portrait. It reminded her of someone, but she couldn't put her finger on who. Hazel lingered on the drawing for a while, but nothing came to her. She resumed reading.

I happened across Mercy Frump in the orchard today. She was unaware of my presence and I did not wish to disturb her as it seemed to me she was lost in a reverie of sorts, some quiet contemplation—perhaps prayer. Her head was bowed and her lips were moving, but she made no sound. I turned to go but something stayed me. Then I saw it: the hawk. It swooped down from above, silent but for the noise of its wings. It alighted on the branch of the tree nearest the lady and seemed to wait. She raised her head and stared at the bird a moment. Then she held out her hand and the hawk settled itself on her arm. I do not know how its talons failed to pierce the sleeve of her coat. The scene was so strange it brought a mist over my eyes and I felt faint, as if the earth had shifted beneath my feet. I stumbled, and in so doing snapped a twig underfoot. The noise rang out like rifle shot. When I looked toward Mistress Frump to make my apologies, she had vanished, along with the hawk. Did I imagine it all?

Huh. Looks like there's always been something strange about the hawks near Land's End, Hazel reflected. She read on eagerly, but the next few entries didn't mention Mercy or the hawk. Instead, Diary Guy talked about missing his family and about rumours in the village about possible Fenian raids. Diary Guy was supposed to meet one of the Fenian leaders at a place called the Rose & River Inn, and present him with a gift from his family, something that would help mount another invasion of Canada. But Diary Guy sounded nervous about the whole idea. He seemed to be worried he might lose the gift he was carrying, before he even had a chance to hand it over. And that would get him into big trouble with his family.

The more Hazel read, the clearer it became that Diary Guy wasn't interested in any disputes between the Irish and British. He really just wanted everyone in the New World to get along. He was more concerned with trying to capture on canvas the expression of one Edwin Cornelius Frump without making his smile appear too sinister.

"Hey! You're *that* guy—the one who painted that portrait." Hazel set the diary down. She stared at the painting of Edwin Frump. There was a signature on the bottom left corner of the portrait, but she'd been unable to decipher it. Would this diary give her the painter's name? And would he ever explain why he'd hidden this diary in the library?

My belongings continue to disappear. I cannot think what has become of them. At first I believed I was merely forgetful and had misplaced the items. After a while, when they failed to reappear, I began to wonder if I had simply imagined their existence in the first place. But such a strange assortment of personal trappings . . . Why would I dream of a pocket knife, a handkerchief, a watch fob or a paintbrush? Yet, how could I mislay such things? I turn in for the night, leaving my shoes by the chest of drawers, and when I awake in the morn, the shoes are exactly where I placed them but a lace is missing! I begin to wonder if this castle, so newly constructed, could already be haunted. For surely it must be spirits or ghosts making mischief here. My hosts are odd, it is true, but I cannot believe a member of the Frump family would prove a thief.

The next entry made Hazel sit up.

I am losing sleep. I cannot trust my eyes or ears. Something is terribly wrong in this house. At night my dreams are fevered and confused. By morning I am worn and weary—it is as if I tossed all night without rest. This sounds incredible but I awoke three days ago to find that someone had cut a lock of my hair while I slept. I thought perhaps a mouse had nibbled it away, but then this morning I awoke to find my nails had been shorn to the quick. Am I imagining it, or is there a spirit at work here? Perhaps there is a ghost or some such creature that comes and spies on me in my bed . . . I hear noises but when I wake no one is there.

My nerves are so strained that my fancies continue even during daylit hours. I walk the corridors of this castle and feel eyes upon my back. When I turn around, the hallway is always empty. I have sewn pockets into all my clothing that I may always carry my family's gift with me—woe betide me if I should ever lose it. Thank heaven the paintings I have been commissioned to create are nearly done. I count the days until I may take my leave of this strange place.

Never before have I believed in spirits or witchcraft, yet now I begin to wonder.

Hazel couldn't have stopped reading now if the castle had caught on fire. She sped through the next few entries, which dealt mostly with the painter's difficulty in capturing the likeness of Edwin Frump and his eagerness to be gone. A few more entries followed, consisting mostly of complaints about how little sleep the painter was getting and the technical problems he was having as he hurried to complete a painting of Land's End itself. But the next section grabbed Hazel's attention.

I was stunned to learn today that it is the lady Mercy who has been taking my things. Her elder brother, Edwin, confessed that she suffers from a malady that compels her to purloin the belongings of others. Shiny objects are particularly appealing to her, and I suppose this explains my missing watch fob and pocket knife. (Although the taking of the shoelace, I must admit, I find perplexing.) It is a disquieting revelation, yet I am relieved to learn the explanation for my sleeplessness—for how could anyone rest comfortably when a stranger is stealing into his room by night to remove personal effects and tokens? Naturally, the Frump family has tried to preserve Mercy's reputation. It seems she began thieving when only a child. Edwin spoke of his fear that I might now expose his sister's secret, but I assured him that I will say nothing. I asked only that my belongings be returned to me, and my commission paid as soon as possible. The paintings are finished and I am anxious to complete my task for the Fenian Brotherhood and return home. I harbour no ill-will toward that poor woman.

So Mercy was a kleptomaniac! Hazel shook her head. The Frumps had nerve: building a castle and commissioning portraits, as if they were some kind of royalty, and all the time, behind the scenes, they're stealing shoelaces!

"People are funny," Hazel announced to the empty room.

But the next entry wasn't funny at all. The next entry made Hazel's blood run cold.

CHAPTER ELEVEN

The spidery handwriting now appeared rushed and Diary Guy's frantic words practically leapt off the page as Hazel, her pulse racing, read on:

Edwin Cornelius Frump is an evil man. I do not trust him. He is a liar of fearsome skill, and moreover he has a twisted soul. How do I know these things to be true?

Yesterday I came across Mercy while walking in the walled garden. We talked for some time. At first we spoke of inconsequential things, but she soon revealed herself to be both intelligent and charming. I could not reconcile the troubled thief her brother had described with the lovely woman who stood before me. Somehow I found the courage to broach the topic of my purloined belongings. Mercy was shocked and immediately denied her brother's account. When I pressed for an explanation, she shook her head and appeared to fight back tears.

At first I was skeptical. Whom should I believe—the brother or the sister?

So Hazel had been right about Creepy Edwin all along. But why was Diary Guy hesitating?

"Come on, trust Mercy," she muttered. "He may be my own ancestor, but even I can see Edwin's rotten to the core."

The longer I spoke to Mercy, the clearer it became that she was indeed of sound mind. What would cause her brother to invent such a wicked tale? He surely would not try to protect a servant by casting blame upon his sister. Could it be Edwin himself who stole my things?

"Well, duh." Impatience coursed through Hazel's veins. If Diary Guy were here, she'd shake him until his teeth rattled. "Wake up!"

It is true I have felt uncomfortable around Edwin all along. Something about him disturbs me. Try as I have to paint a flattering portrait of the man, his expression betrays him.

I passed the night in restlessness and by morning I could not stand it any longer. I sought out Mercy again and demanded an explanation for my missing belongings. When I listed the items taken from my room, the colour drained from Mercy's cheeks and she advised me to leave Land's End at once. I begged her to explain, but she would say only that I was in grave danger. She was greatly taken aback to learn I had not yet been paid. I could see her turning the matter over in her mind. Finally she asked to meet me in the chapel the next morning and promised that there she would settle the Frump debt in full "with extra for your troubles," if only I would depart immediately thereafter and never return to Land's End.

I told her I would be only too happy to quit this place.

Despite her reticence I found myself confiding in her, explaining the errand my family has entrusted to me. I even showed her the gift I carry for the Fenian Brotherhood. She has no love for the Fenians, but respects the bonds of family. She told me I was wise to sew the pockets and bade me carry the precious gift always, lest it disappear in the manner of my other belongings.

I have agreed to meet Mercy in the chapel. But will tomorrow truly see me bid farewell to this strange place?

Hazel's stomach was grumbling, but this was no time to break for food. She had to find out what happened next. What kind of "grave danger" was Mercy talking about? She turned the page and stared in disbelief. Gibberish! Diary Guy had kept writing but not in any language Hazel recognized. The last entries were filled with letters strung together in a way that made no sense at all. She flipped hurriedly past them, but the rest of the book was blank.

It took every ounce of restraint Hazel possessed not to hurl the book across the room. But she did allow herself a massive groan.

"Uh, Hazel? Am I interrupting something?"

Matt was standing in the doorway, a look of concern on his face.

Hazel bolted upright, dropping the diary on the floor.

"Wow, Matt, I didn't hear you come in. When did you get home?"

"Just now. I brought some laundry, figured I'd stick around for the weekend, get a break from all the noise and partying . . ." His voice trailed away. "You know, I never realized it before, but even compared to the libraries at my university, this is a pretty amazing room."

"Yeah." Privately, Hazel told herself Matt had no idea how amazing the library was.

"It's almost dinnertime, and Deirdre just called to say she's on her way home with the kids, from that maze. Dad said you were doing homework, so I said I'd come get you. How's that history assignment coming along, anyway?"

Hazel liked the way Matt lumped Ned and Oliver together as *the kids*. But any illusion she had of belonging among the older cousins was shattered when Matt asked about her homework. He was *such* a big brother.

"Fine." She shrugged, picking up the diary and the sketches she'd removed from the folder.

Matt glanced quizzically at the empty library tables and undisturbed bookcases. But as he led the way out of the room, all he said was, "Yeah, looks like you've been hitting the books hard."

The intoxicating smell of warm chocolate hit her nostrils as soon as Hazel opened the kitchen door. The scene that met her eyes reminded her of the summer. Oliver was drinking a glass of milk and Deirdre was laughing at something Ned had said and the radio was blaring "The Ride of the Valkyries" at an ear-splitting decibel-level. Mark was at the stove, stirring a giant pot of his homemade chili. He must have been there a while, Hazel guessed, because he was surrounded by trays of freshly baked chocolate chip cookies, and, cooling on a rack beside them, two pans of chocolate cake. Mark's eyes were closed and he was humming along with the music.

"Hey, Mark!" Hazel hollered over the music. "I didn't know you were home too!"

Mark opened his eyes. "Hey, cousin!" He waved his wooden spoon at her, spattering chili across the floor.

Oliver waved hello too, and his arm knocked over a giant

can of olive oil, sending a tidal wave of the stuff streaming across the floor. Ned jumped up to avoid the spill, knocking over two chairs. As Deirdre bent over to pick them up, Mark did the same and their heads clunked together like something out of a cartoon.

"Ohhhhhhh." Mark grabbed his forehead and pretended to swoon. "I think I see stars."

Oliver burst into laughter, snorting milk out of his nose.

"Eew. That is disgusting. Oliver, YOU are disgusting. Clean that up, for Pete's sake." Deirdre grabbed a cloth from the kitchen counter and tossed it at her younger brother. She missed and hit Mark in the neck. Mark whipped the damp cloth back at his sister, hitting her on the head.

"Freeze!" Matt waded into the fray, holding his hands up in the air, palms facing out like a police officer directing traffic. "Everybody just calm down. And somebody, please, turn that music off."

For a moment it worked. Everyone stopped. And then, shockingly, Matt skidded in the oil slick, his legs sliding out from under him as his arms windmilled uselessly through the air. There was a moment's silence when he landed heavily on his back. Then everyone started forward at once, asking if he was okay.

"Stay where you are!" Matt's right arm shot out. "I mean it: nobody move. Don't even think of helping me . . . you clowns."

At that moment, Uncle Seamus walked in. His head bent over some documents, he appeared oblivious to the chaos. For Hazel, the next few seconds seemed to unfold in slow motion. She saw Uncle Seamus's foot slip on the oil, heard Matt warn, "Look out!" and Mark call, "Man down!" There was no time to save Uncle Seamus—Matt was still on the floor, he'd cushion the fall—so Hazel concentrated on the folder, diving for it as it flew out of her uncle's hands, and catching it inches above the ground.

"Reflexes like a cat!" Mark crowed. "Another beautiful save by Hazel Frump, ladies and gentlemen!"

It took a few minutes before order was restored. And even after the oil had been mopped up and the chairs set to rights and Mark had handed around a calming plate of cookies that he called hors d'oeuvres, Matt could still be heard muttering something about the Three Stooges.

"I was going to ask if you children would be all right if I left town for a few days," Uncle Seamus said. "But I'm beginning to wonder if that would be wise."

Uncle Seamus explained that he needed to fly to Edmonton for a legal case he was handling for an important client. Matt stopped grumbling and quickly offered to stay at Land's End and commute to university for classes.

"Me too," Mark said. "Except for the commuting part. I wasn't intending to go back to Montreal on Sunday anyway. I've got a bit of a break right now, and I actually came home to get some studying done in peace and quiet."

Uncle Seamus looked at him curiously. "You came *here* for peace and quiet?"

"It's hard to believe, I know," Mark said. "But I have a loud, very chatty roommate and a very small dorm room; it will be way easier to work at home."

"It *is* hard to believe," Uncle Seamus said.

After dinner, when the dishes had all been washed and the kitchen floor mopped one more time, Uncle Seamus headed to his room to pack. After agreeing to meet later in one of the games rooms for a darts tournament, the cousins went their separate ways—to do laundry, study, read or e-mail friends. Hazel was anxious to tell Ned about the diary and the sketches, but before she could say anything, he'd grabbed her arm and dragged her upstairs to the privacy of her room.

As soon as they'd closed the door behind them, Hazel and Ned both began babbling at once. Ned finally held up a hand.

"One at a time, okay?"

Hazel nodded.

"Great. Me first," Ned said. "I have to tell you about what I found out at the corn maze."

"We solved that clue already," Hazel began, but subsided at a look from her brother.

"It's called the Maize Maze." Ned pulled a crumpled pamphlet from his pocket and handed it to Hazel. "That gives you information about mazes and labyrinths and explains how they have to plant this thing every year. It's going to come down in a few days—that's why Deirdre and Oliver were in such a hurry to show me. Anyway, it's pretty big and it has lots of dead ends and stuff just like you'd expect. In some places, there are holes through the corn rows, where little kids panicked or decided to cheat or whatever, and take a shortcut. But mostly the corn is really high and thick and you can't see through to the next path. But, sometimes you can *hear*." Ned paused for dramatic emphasis.

Hazel shrugged. "Hear what? The corn growing?"

"Other people." Ned lowered his voice, even though they were alone. "I was trying to keep close to Oliver, but he ran into a friend from school, and they got talking about some science quiz, so when I stopped to tie my shoe, they didn't notice. And while I was kneeling there, I heard *them*, on the other side of the corn."

"Okay, I'll play. Who did you hear?"

"Kenny Pritchard and his old pal Billy!"

"Are you sure? I thought Kenny was supposed to be grounded until he was around thirty-six," Hazel said.

"It was Kenny, all right. He was talking about his dad and his uncle being in jail and everything. And then he started talking about Charlotte, and how she's been coming around, talking to his mum. And, Hazel, he knows about the treasure hunt!"

"Kenny?" Hazel shook her head in disbelief. "No way, you must have heard wrong."

Ned made a growling sound. "Trust me. Charlotte's been talking about it with Kenny's mum, like . . . I don't know, an example of how 'parenting' can be fun or something."

"So, did Charlotte tell Kenny about it too?" Hazel was struggling not to feel betrayed. She didn't like the idea of Charlotte talking about it behind their backs with Kenny.

"No. I think Kenny just overheard Charlotte and his mum talking about it," Ned said. "Charlotte was worried about some of the places she had to hide clues, and she asked Kenny's mum for advice."

"What kind of worried? Like, worried the hiding places are too easy, or worried they're too hard?" Hazel frowned.

"I don't know."

"Huh." Hazel looked at Ned. "I don't like the idea of Kenny knowing what we're doing, and making fun of it with his friends."

"Yeah, and I don't like the idea that Uncle Seamus and Charlotte believe he's really grounded," Ned said. "Grown-ups are so gullible."

"What was Kenny doing at the corn maze, anyway? That doesn't sound like his kind of place."

"I don't think he was actually in the maze itself. I'm pretty sure I was beside one of the outside walls of corn when I heard them," Ned said. "The Maize Maze is right next door to a park with one of those pioneer villages . . . maybe they sneaked in through the park."

"My turn." Hazel showed Ned the painter's diary, and the sketches of Mercy and the hawk. They retrieved the box of jewels from under the window seat, where Hazel had stored them for safekeeping.

"There's no doubt about it," Ned said, holding the sapphire pin beside the sketch. "It's a match."

"But we still don't know what it means." Hazel traced the drawing of Mercy lightly with her finger. "I mean, did Dad hide these jewels for us to find? Or are they the lost jewels?"

"I dunno. But I do know one thing: you were right."

"About what?"

"It's the third thing." Using his fingers, Ned ticked off the list. "We found the spell book in the library and the jewels, and you said there should be a third thing, like in fairy tales. And now you found it: the diary."

"You don't look so happy about it," Hazel observed.

"It's not that." Ned sprang up from his chair and began to pace the room. "It's just weird to think I'm named for that creepy guy in the portrait. Do you think he was really spying on Diary Guy and taking his stuff?"

"Oh. I forgot that Ned is short for Edwin." Hazel tilted her head and considered her brother. "Come to think of it, you do look a little like the portrait."

"Nice. I bet there's a portrait in an attic somewhere of an ancestor named Hazel who's even uglier."

There was a knock on the door and Mark's voice called out, "Hey, Frumps, let's go: we've got sharp, pointy objects and a kid with no aim—that would be young Oliver—oh yes, it's darts played like you've never played before! To the death! Or at least, the dismemberment!"

Ned grinned. "I guess we'd better go."

There was no chance for Hazel and Ned to talk further that night, and breakfast the next morning was a crowded affair. The entire family descended on the kitchen simultaneously, drawn by the aroma of Mark's blueberry pancakes and bacon. Hazel wanted to search the library for more information about Creepy Edwin, Diary Guy and Mercy, but Ned had his sights set on the next clue. Before Hazel could say anything, he had wrangled them a ride into the village. Matt, who was driving Uncle Seamus to the train station, would drop them off at the park. Mark would pick them up later in the truck, along with Deirdre (who wouldn't leave the house without showering and shampooing her hair).

"But why do you need to practise basketball at the public court when we put up that perfectly good hoop right here on the tennis court?" Uncle Seamus asked.

Mark grinned. "Uh, maybe it's because the public court has hoops at *both* ends of the court, Dad."

Ned had confided his plan to Oliver, and they'd agreed he could come, so long as he didn't help. But when they reached the park with the basketball court, Hazel could tell that Oliver had his own theory about the clue, and was bursting to confide it.

"So, 'Behind my door / There is a store / (A clock)' and, uh, what was the other thing?" Oliver pretended to search his memory.

"Troops marching in a hurry." Ned began to poke around the shrubbery. "Maybe we need to find a war memorial or something."

Oliver appeared to cough into his sleeve, but Hazel was pretty sure she caught the word *store*. Looking around, she spotted a colourful shopfront on the north side of the street. An oversize clock hung above the entrance.

"Hey, Ned, look over there." Hazel pointed. "Check out that store with the crazy door."

"McCormack's Models," Ned read aloud. "Hey, like model soldiers? Little toy troops?"

"And trains." Oliver radiated satisfaction.

Hazel smothered a grin. "Let's go." She led the way across the park, but Oliver drew back.

"The thing is," Oliver said, "the guy who owns that store is really mean. He hates kids. If you don't mind, I think I'd rather not go in."

After some discussion Hazel and Ned agreed they would meet Oliver at the tea shop up the street once they'd retrieved the clue. As soon as Oliver had gone, Ned and Hazel raced across the road to McCormack's Models. It was impossible to believe the owner of a shop that looked like this could hate kids. Now that they were close enough to see properly, Ned pointed out that the giant clock had bayonets for arms and soldiers instead of numbers. Even the wooden door was enticing; painted carvings of steam engines covered almost every inch of its eight-foot height. Below their feet, a welcome mat was decorated with images of cannons and soldiers. Hazel stared at the mat, her pulse quickening. Wasn't that an envelope sticking out from underneath?

But when she bent to retrieve it, only the corner of an envelope was there. And before Hazel could examine it closely, the wind tore it from her fingers and tossed it high into the air, before sending it dancing down the street amid a swirl of dry leaves.

"This has got to be the place, Hazel." Ned's face was pressed against the windowpane. On the other side of the glass someone had arranged an intricate display of model trains running in and around an old fort. British and French soldiers were arrayed on a hill behind it. Everything had been built to an exacting scale.

"I see lots of soldiers." Ned sighed. "How are we going to know which one is hiding the clue?"

"We'll have to go in and look around, silly. It can't be that bad. I'm sure Oliver was exaggerating."

But the moment they entered the shop, Hazel knew they had made a terrible mistake. Ned's gaze flitted from one dazzling display to another, but Hazel only had eyes for the heavy-set man scowling behind the counter, and his very large dog.

"Hello." Hazel gave her most polite smile, tucking her hands behind her back. "Do you mind if we look around?"

The dog gave a low, ominous growl. The man said nothing, but as he stepped around to the front of the counter, he cracked his knuckles.

"Uh, we were just looking for a present for our uncle. He likes trains. Model trains, I mean. We couldn't help noticing you have a lot of them."

"I don't like kids," the man said.

"I—I, uh, I beg your pardon?" Hazel stammered.

"Don't like kids. They come in with their food and their drinks and they drop their wrappers on my floor and make noise and mess up the displays, and they steal. Don't like kids."

"Oh. Right. Well, never mind then. We'll just be going." Hazel turned her back on the odd man and made a face at Ned.

"C'mon," she whispered.

But Ned gave an almost imperceptible jerk of his head toward the display just beside him. There, jutting out from behind a tree that was sheltering several model soldiers was a small, square envelope—a clue-sized envelope.

Great. How were they supposed to retrieve that without knocking over half the display? If she so much as lifted a finger to touch one of the soldiers, the shopkeeper would strangle her with his bare hands and feed her to his dog. What were Charlotte and Dad *thinking*?

But Ned had stepped past her and was talking in a low, soothing voice. At first Hazel thought he was speaking to the dog. But it was the man Ned was trying to charm.

"My dad used to have some American Flyers and some

Lionels. I've seen an Ives at my uncle's. Do you prefer the HO gauge or the Hornby 00 gauge?"

The man made a sound somewhere between a grunt and a sigh. Hazel's jaw dropped. How did Ned know so much about trains? But Ned had one hand behind his back and was waggling his fingers at her. She sidled closer to the display.

This was no time for finesse. Hazel yanked on the corner of the envelope. Within seconds the clue was out from under the tree and in her pocket. But as the shopkeeper turned to face her, Hazel heard a sound. It was the sound of a tree falling in the display. And knocking over another tree. And another. Out of the corner of her eye, Hazel could see an entire forest tumbling down a long slope of artificial turf, just as a tiny steam engine came hurtling around the corner. Ned leaped forward to block the trees from falling across the tracks, a nanosecond before the engine hurtled past.

"All clear," Ned said, panting slightly. He set the trees down, patting them gently. "See? No harm, no foul."

"You . . . you . . ." The shopkeeper raised a trembling finger. The enormous dog bared its teeth.

Ned grabbed Hazel's hand. "Run."

CHAPTER TWELVE

Panting and out of breath, Hazel and Ned sprawled across one of the painted wooden benches that overlooked the marina. The shopkeeper from McCormack's Models had followed them to the door, letting his snarling dog give chase while he watched, hollering and shaking his fist. The dog didn't quit until Hazel and Ned reached the farthest end of the park, but just to be safe, they kept running until they got to the boardwalk that separated the park from the marina.

Hazel closed her eyes and listened to the cheerful noises of the harbour—seagulls calling overhead, the waves lapping against the hull of a boat, a distant bell clanging in the wind, a small motorboat chugging toward the breakwater. A light breeze tickled her skin.

"You feeling all right, Hazel? You have this dopey look on your face."

Hazel opened her eyes to see that Ned had thrown his head back in imitation of her. With eyes closed and a dreamy smile, he did, indeed, look dopey.

"Very funny."

"Not as funny as the look on your face when you knocked over that display. Who knew you were such a klutz?"

"Hey, it's not my fault Dad—or Charlotte—put the envelope there. We could have gotten in a lot of trouble."

"Yeah." The teasing look had disappeared from Ned's eyes. "Strange, eh?"

"Very strange. I wonder if . . ." Hazel pulled the envelope from her pocket. It was badly crumpled but all four corners were intact. "No, never mind. For a moment I thought maybe someone had moved the clue, because I found a torn bit of envelope outside, under the welcome mat. But this envelope is whole."

"Still, it's a good point," Ned said. "Charlotte could have put the envelope somewhere else, and it just got moved. Or maybe she was in a hurry, so she just dumped the clue in that display and took off. She never likes to keep a sick cow waiting."

Hazel nodded. "Maybe she's not that into this treasure hunt. The other clues were written in that fancy handwriting, but this one is typed.

Ned shrugged. "Yeah, or maybe Charlotte can't do fancy writing like Dad. Open it, will you? The suspense is killing me."

The paper Hazel drew from the envelope was remarkably ordinary—no fancy colours or textures. She read aloud:

A beacon of light that was never extinguished,
(Hospitality that's far from distinguished),
I'm under a welcome mat not far away,
"A pillar of fire by night, of cloud by day."
Think of a sailor seeking safe passage
(Or a sandwich that's sadly no better than average).

"Strange." Ned plucked the clue from Hazel's hands to read it for himself.

"It sounds sort of like a lighthouse," Hazel said slowly. "You know, with sailors seeking safe passage, and a beacon of light and everything. But I don't really get the part about the hospitality."

"Or the lame sandwich." Ned handed the clue back to her, his face glum. "Looks like we'll be Googling another poem. Maybe you were right, and we should concentrate more on the ancient mystery."

Hazel smiled at his use of the word *ancient*. It had been little more than a hundred years since Edwin and Mercy Frump had walked the halls of Land's End. And lately, they had begun to feel as real to Hazel as Deirdre and Oliver.

"Hey, look at the time!" Ned grabbed Hazel's arm. "We'd better get to the tea shop to meet Oliver—we don't want him looking for us at McCormack's Models!"

But Oliver was calmly drinking a milkshake when Hazel and Ned sank into the booth, breathless and full of apologies.

"That's okay." Oliver looked them over. "Did you find the next clue?"

For answer, Hazel showed him the envelope.

Ned sighed. "It's not fair. This would be so much more fun if we could include you."

"Don't feel bad—I'm used to secrets. I've got one big sister and two big brothers. Nobody ever tells me anything."

Hazel smiled. "I think you do a pretty good job of finding out stuff on your own."

After leaving the tea shop, the three Frumps walked toward the basketball court, where they had arranged to meet Mark and Deirdre. They paused in front of the art and antiques shop owned by Clive Pritchard.

"It's been closed since he was arrested," Oliver said quietly.

"I think the police are supposed to be checking everything in Mr. Pritchard's homes in case it's stuff that's stolen or fake, but they haven't got to this store yet."

Hazel peered through the dust and grime that coated the leaded-glass window. The painting that Ned had identified in the summer as a work by Paolo Cafazzo was still there, surrounded by a jumble of old books, Victorian footstools and silverware. Ned nudged her and pointed.

Hazel gasped. High on the wall near the window was what looked to be a very old portrait of a beautiful woman. She was dressed in the same type of long gown Mercy Frump wore in her portrait, but there the resemblance ended. This woman was younger and wore a cruel, gloating expression. Her hands were crossed in front of her dress and one finger wore an enormous ruby ring.

The ring from the library.

"Hey, Oliver," Ned said, and Hazel could hear the effort it took to keep the excitement out of his voice. "Do you know anything about that painting up there?"

"Oh, that?" Oliver shrugged. "Just that it's always been there. People say a rich American wanted to buy it once, but it's the only thing in the shop Mr. Pritchard won't sell—no matter how much you offer."

"Why?" Hazel said.

"Nobody knows," Oliver said. "I think she might be some kind of ancestor of the Pritchards. She reminds me a bit of Kenny."

That could just be the expression on her face, Hazel thought.

"Personally you couldn't pay me enough to keep that thing on my wall." Ned's lip curled in disgust. "She's pretty and everything, but she looks mean. Creepy, even."

As creepy as Edwin Frump, Hazel thought.

When they reached the park and the basketball court, Hazel cast a nervous eye toward McCormack's Models. But the shop's window shades had been pulled down and a Closed sign hung on the door.

"Too much excitement for one day," Ned murmured at her elbow.

When Deirdre and Mark showed up, they all spent a few minutes dribbling and shooting. Deirdre was getting better, Hazel noted approvingly. But Mark was still hopeless.

"That was one of the worst air balls I've ever seen!" Hazel said, as Mark's shot missed the basket by about ten feet.

"I resent your stereotype. Just because I'm tall doesn't mean I play basketball," Mark said in a lofty tone. "I'll have you know I'm always picked first in soccer *and* in Ultimate Frisbee."

"It's true," Deirdre said, laughing. "But show her what happens when you *try* to miss."

Oliver ran to the baseline, some fifteen feet out from the basket. Mark faced Oliver, screwing up his forehead in concentration. He lofted the ball high in the air and it sailed on a flawless trajectory, straight to the hoop, grazing the backboard slightly before dropping through the net.

"Neat trick," Hazel acknowledged. "It really looked like you were aiming for Oliver."

"Oh, it's no trick, my friend," Mark said sorrowfully. "C'mon, let's go do the shopping."

Matt's car was in the driveway when they returned to Land's End. He met them on the porch and helped carry in groceries.

"I hear there was some kind of trouble in the village this morning—at McCormack's store," he said. "Did you see what happened?"

Oliver fumbled his bag of apples, nearly spilling them onto the lawn.

Ned choked on nothing and began coughing. Hazel thumped his back energetically. "Sorry—you okay, Ned?—where was this, uh, trouble?"

"McCormack's Models. They sell model trains and planes and old toy soldiers. I heard some kids tried to vandalize it. But you never know with McCormack's. The guy who owns it is a bit of a crank. Hates kids. He's some kind of distant relative of the Pritchards."

Hazel felt as if something was crawling up her skin. "Seriously? He's related to Clive and Kenny?"

"Well, not the Pritchard side of that family—I'm pretty sure he's related to Kenny's mum somehow. In fact, I don't think he and Clive get along. Kenny sometimes works in the store, though."

"If he hates kids, why does Kenny work there?" Ned asked.

Matt set his bags down on the kitchen table and turned to go back for more. "Dunno. Maybe Kenny's dad makes him. He's the kind of guy who thinks yelling's good for kids."

"Maybe Kenny's the reason the guy hates kids," Ned muttered. But Matt was already gone.

After the groceries were unpacked, Oliver beckoned Hazel and Ned to follow him to his room. From under his bed, he pulled out a padded canvas bag and unzipped it to reveal a laptop computer.

"I don't really mind you using my computer, but I thought you might like one of your own. It's not very new but it works fine, and with the wireless connection you can get the Internet anywhere at Land's End. And you can still print things off on my printer."

Hazel threw her arms around Oliver and kissed the top of his head. Ned punched his shoulder lightly.

"Thanks, guy. Hey, do you mind if we . . ." Ned looked uncertainly from Oliver to Hazel and back again.

"I'd go to Hazel's room if I were you," Oliver said. "More privacy."

Googling the phrase in quotation marks along with the word *poem* produced the answer in seconds. Henry Wadsworth Longfellow had written the line, in a poem called "The Lighthouse."

"It's so simple it's crazy." Ned leaned back in his chair, arms clasped behind his head. "We find a lighthouse and look under the welcome mat."

"There's probably more than one lighthouse on the island, though. I'm pretty sure there's one near the village. And there's one on the other side of the island —you can see it from the ferry, remember?"

"Whoa!" Ned sprang up as if he'd been pricked by a pin. "There's one right here, too. On the grounds of Land's End, remember? Deirdre told us about it in the summer. It was built just after the castle, and the light doesn't work anymore, but Uncle Seamus restored the house and keeps it as a guest house."

Hazel's cheeks flamed. She felt incredibly slow.

"Oh yeah. I forgot."

"So? Let's go!"

"No, I meant I forgot about the lighthouse before, during the storm, when I was lost in the woods. I could have taken shelter there."

Ned looked at her. "You were *lost*, silly. You were wandering around, sick as a dog, and it's not like there was a sign saying, LIGHTHOUSE THIS WAY."

Hazel couldn't help laughing. "True."

Ned wanted to set off for the lighthouse immediately, but Hazel pointed out that it was already dark, and nearly time for dinner. They argued for a few minutes but common sense was on Hazel's side and even Ned could see it.

Mark had baked his own bread to go with dinner and he was

lifting the warm, crusty loaves from the oven just as Charlotte was ladling spaghetti onto plates. It gave Hazel a familiar cozy feeling to sit at the enormous kitchen table with all of her cousins talking at once. But she was starting to wonder about all the secrets they were keeping.

"So, were you kids near McCormack's Models today when the Attack of the Vandals occurred?" Charlotte asked.

"I heard some kids made quite a mess in there," Matt said. "Not locals, though. No one seems to know who it was."

Charlotte tilted her head to one side and looked at Ned, who was busy twirling spaghetti and trying not to look at her.

"I heard it was a boy and a girl," she said, her voice tentative.

Hazel shot a sidelong glance at Ned. Ned set his fork down with an air of great restraint.

"I heard it was a couple of kids on a treasure hunt." Ned looked Charlotte straight in the eye. "But the clue was impossible to reach without knocking over this whole display, and that's why the kids got in trouble."

"Wait. The treasure hunt took you *inside* McCormack's Models?" Confusion wrinkled Charlotte's brow. "You didn't find it outside?"

Ned shook his head. "Inside."

Mark gave a low whistle. "Talk about dangerous—that McCormack guy is one crabby dude. You're lucky you got out of there alive!"

Charlotte was about to speak, when the phone rang. She answered it in a distracted way, but instantly snapped to attention, her face grave. Seconds later, she was reaching for her coat.

"I've got to go—a very ill foal needs my help. But I'll be back first thing in the morning because we need to talk about this, okay?"

They never got to have that talk.

The next morning, when Hazel joined Ned, Oliver and Deirdre in the kitchen, they found Matt and Mark sitting slumped across the breakfast table from each other, eyes downcast, fingers wrapped around forgotten cups of coffee, staring at nothing.

"What's wrong?" Deirdre darted forward immediately. "What's happened?"

Matt blinked and shook his head slightly, as if clearing it. "We've got some bad news."

Ned made an involuntary movement, and Matt's gaze shifted from his sister. "It's okay, Ned, Hazel, it's not Uncle Colin or Dad. They're both fine."

"It's Charlotte," Mark said, turning to face them. "There's been some sort of accident. She's in the hospital."

CHAPTER THIRTEEN

"Kinda breezy, eh?" Hazel turned to face Ned, but the wind whipped her words away as soon as she spoke. "At least we're nearly there."

"What?" Ned hollered.

It was good to be outside, good to be doing something. Sunday had been a miserable day spent hanging around at the hospital, waiting for Charlotte to wake up. No one was really sure what had happened. She had offered to stay with the sick foal overnight, something she often did. But when the horse trainer had brought her coffee at dawn, he'd found Charlotte lying unconscious in the stable, and called 911.

At first they'd all assumed a horse had kicked Charlotte, or that she'd fallen and hit her head. But the horse trainer told the police he suspected someone else had been in the barn that night. So the police were waiting for Charlotte to wake up too.

In the end, the hospital had sent them all away.

When Matt and Mark called Uncle Seamus, he'd wanted to cut short his business trip. But the twins persuaded him that there was nothing he could do for Charlotte. In the meantime, the three of them decided Monday should be as normal as possible, under the circumstances. Matt had dropped Deirdre and Oliver at school before continuing on to the university for a class. And Mark had gone to the hospital to visit Charlotte. Both twins expected to be back at Land's End by mid-afternoon; in the meantime, Hazel and Ned had promised to stay out of trouble.

They had little time to waste, then, if they wanted to get to the lighthouse and back again before Matt or Mark returned. But Ned had insisted on packing what he called "contingency rations" (Hazel called them "snacks") and topping up his pack with a random assortment of things like flashlights, rope, duct tape, matches and a compass.

"A compass?" Hazel had asked.

"You never know, the next clue could tell us to face west and take so many paces and then south and so many paces."

"It's not a pirate writing the clues—it's Dad," Hazel had said. "And if we walked west and south from the lighthouse we'd end up in the lake."

Ned was a funny combination of genius and regular boy. But watching him now, head down, staggering into the wind, Hazel was awfully glad they were together again.

For the first time, it occurred to her that Charlotte had no brothers or sisters. Maybe that was why she never seemed to mind looking after the cousins. Hazel swallowed, remembering Charlotte's tight embrace after the paintball attack, and how she had stayed at the castle until Uncle Seamus got home, baking muffins and making sure Hazel felt safe.

Charlotte was bigger than Hazel but in her hospital bed she'd seemed so small and fragile. Ned had entered the drab room quickly, kissed Charlotte's cheek and returned to the waiting room in a matter of seconds. Hazel knew he was overwhelmed by the whole scene.

But she hadn't been able to leave Charlotte, not until the nurse insisted. She just sat there quietly, watching her breathe. Charlotte was breathing on her own—she didn't need any machines to help, and the doctor had said that was important. Deirdre had chatted away as if Charlotte could hear, while Hazel had watched the slow, steady rise and fall of her chest. One side of Charlotte's face was swollen and bruised and blood had seeped through some of the bandages. But she was breathing. She would keep breathing. And she'd wake up. Soon.

"Don't just stand there," Ned barked, pushing past her. "Onward, ho!"

"Onward, ho? What have you been reading?" Hazel muttered. But she fell in step beside him.

They should see the lighthouse any moment. They had already passed through Big Sandy Bay and the cove with the entrance to the smugglers' tunnels. Hazel's stomach had twisted, remembering her endless journey through the woods. But today the sky was the colour of a robin's egg, and the sun on her skin felt like a gift.

"Could be worse," Ned shouted up at her. "Could be raining."

Hazel smiled. Then she caught Ned's sleeve and pointed.

"There it is—see? Just around the next cove."

But the lighthouse wasn't just around the next cove. Hazel and Ned soon discovered that coastlines could be deceiving. No sooner had they rounded the bay than they found themselves in another inlet, with the lighthouse still beckoning from a farther point.

They were both dragging their feet by the time they reached the rocky promontory where the lighthouse stood. The wind had made the hike seem twice as long, and Hazel had a feeling it was the sort of wind that managed never to be at your back. The walk home would feel just as long.

At least the lighthouse was cheery. The massive stone pillar looked more welcoming up close than it had from afar, helped by a cozy cottage that adjoined it. Its rough-hewn stone was whitewashed and gleamed in the sunshine. Someone had painted the cottage's shutters and door a bright red to match the cage at the top of the tower that housed the old light. There were even red window boxes, and though they were empty, the effect was still charming.

"Hey, Hazel? I don't see a welcome mat."

Ned was right. Hazel saw a red wooden door at the base of the tower and another at the front of the cottage. But no mats covered the worn stone steps.

"Maybe there's one inside?"

"Or around the back," Ned said. He set off in search of another entrance, while Hazel tried the front door. It wasn't locked, but the wood had swollen and stuck. Just as she wrenched it open, Ned gave a cry.

Hazel raced around the side of the house and almost collided with her brother. "Are you okay?"

Ned nodded. "But just get a load of that. Do you think it happened during that big storm you got trapped in?"

It was as if a giant in steel-toed boots had stomped across the back half of the cottage. Hazel stared at the wreckage. The stone walls were intact, but a big part of the house had obviously been built of wood and it was little more than splinters now. Sections of roof had caved in, and debris was strewn along the shore. Roof tiles were scattered across the rocks like cards in a game of Fifty-Two Pickup.

Ned took a step forward.

"Careful," Hazel warned, "there might be broken glass or nails. Let's use the front door."

"I'm not going inside—are you nuts?" Ned rolled his eyes. "The roof's fallen in and half the walls are busted! I just want to take a look around."

Hazel watched as he picked his way through the debris with exaggerated care.

"Fine." She shrugged her pack off her shoulders and found a spot free of litter where she could sit—a rock the size of a footstool, warmed by the sun and sheltered from the worst of the wind by a much larger boulder. "I'll just sit here and eat some of the snacks—I mean, rations. You go ahead and explore."

"Hey, I'm hungry too."

Hazel rummaged through the pack and pulled out an apple. "Here—catch!"

Ned turned to look, lost his footing and fell backward, disappearing behind a pile of rubble.

"Ned? Are you hurt? Say something!" Hazel leaped to her feet. But when she reached him, she could see from Ned's contemplative expression that he was uninjured. He had landed on an old sofa cushion and was still lying there, staring up at the sky.

"Check out that tower," Ned said.

Hazel turned her face skyward. "It's a lighthouse tower. Made of stone, with a big old busted light at the top. It's pretty, but so what?"

"I think we should investigate it. There might be a welcome mat up there—you know, for tourists."

Hazel squinted.

"Uncle Seamus owns the lighthouse, remember? And even if he opened it to tourists, no one in their right mind would want to climb up there. I'm certainly not going to. You know how I feel about heights."

"You don't have to come." Ned got to his feet, shaking bits of plaster and wood out of his hair.

"Well, I'm not letting you go up there on your own. Look, the clue said a welcome *mat*. I think we should look around down here some more."

Ned rose from his sofa cushion, but Hazel's eye was caught by some yellowed paper wedged inside a piece of wooden wall that was still standing. "Hey, Ned, wait a sec."

"I said you didn't have to come. I'll be back in a minute. Five minutes, tops."

"No, I mean, wait while I get this."

Hazel pried the paper out slowly, taking care not to tear it. It was a newspaper, the *Frontenac Gazette*.

"Wow, the date on this newspaper is July 22, 18—, uh, 18-something-or-other, the ink's blurred. Maybe 1866? 1876?"

"Let me see." Ned took the newspaper from Hazel's outstretched hand. She peered into the wall opening again.

"Hey, there are more papers in here. Hang on while I get them out."

"Why would someone hide newspapers inside a wall?"

"Insulation," Hazel said. "Remember when Dad was renovating that old house in the city, to turn it into a coffee house? There were newspapers in the walls. The paper lasts because it's not really paper. I mean, not the kind that newspapers use today. It was more like cloth. They used rye, I think."

"Uh-huh. Fascinating. Put that in your history assignment. How about I check out that tower now?"

They were certainly accumulating a lot of paper with this mystery, Hazel reflected. She stretched her arm as deep as it could go into the wall cavity. Got it! And there was another, just a little farther in . . . "Ouch!" Hazel didn't want to see the splinter she'd just acquired. Taking a deep breath, she reached in farther until her thumb and forefinger had closed around the corner of another paper. It took longer to wiggle this one free and it tore when the corner snagged on a nail, but in the end she got most of it out.

"There! That makes three newspapers, one diary, one book of spells and a bunch of modern clues. Do you think there's a market for old paper? Maybe we could sell it on eBay! What do you think, Ned? *Ned?*"

He had vanished.

A strange cry tore the air. Hazel darted a glance skyward. A hawk circled the light at the top of the tower.

Hazel gulped. Ned must have gone up the tower without her. And now the hawk wanted her to go too.

"This can't be good," Hazel muttered. Was Ned crazy? From down here the tower looked solid, but who knew how safe it really was. The very thought of climbing all those stairs made her palms sweat.

This would be so much worse than the library catwalk.

She forced her trembling legs to move. Sure enough, the door at the base of the tower was ajar. For a second Hazel hesitated. But this was Ned, her little brother, her only sibling. He was quite possibly the stupidest genius in the whole entire world. But he was *her* stupid genius. She couldn't let anything happen to him.

Hazel knew nothing about lighthouses. She'd pictured an empty cone with a twisting metal staircase winding up, up, up, all the way to the top. To her immense relief, she found actual rooms inside, and the stairs that led from one floor to the next were normal, wooden steps, with a handrail and everything. Steep, but normal.

Still, Hazel tried to not glance down as she climbed. And the higher she climbed, the more light-headed she felt. It wasn't just a fear of heights that made her feel woozy—the temperature seemed to be climbing right along with her, and the air felt thick and stuffy.

Hazel was nearing the top when she heard it. A muffled crash, followed by a sharp cry.

"Oh, Ned, hang on."

The last set of stairs was so steep that it was more like a

ladder, but she pulled herself up. Despite the heat, icy tentacles of dread gripped her heart. Hazel poked her head through the trap door that opened onto the platform at the very top of the tower, and a wave of nausea washed over her. This was high up. Very, very high up. Human beings were not meant to climb this high.

Hazel swallowed. The light was surrounded by windows, massive panes of glass that showed just how far the ground had fallen away beneath her. It took an enormous effort to climb the rest of the way through the opening. She collapsed onto the floor, her cheek resting against the wood. Nice wooden planks. Were they solid? Could she trust them?

From below, the tower hadn't seemed this small. The circular room was so tiny she felt that if she stood in the centre, she might be able to touch both sides.

Hazel forced herself into a kneeling position, gripping the big glass light in the centre of the room for support. She was horribly, impossibly, dangerously high up—but if she looked out to the horizon, far out across the water, maybe . . . Out of nowhere, the hawk swooped past the tower, screaming at her. Hazel jumped.

Ned. She'd been so busy being terrified that she'd almost forgotten him.

But where was he? You couldn't hide a cat in this room, let alone a ten-year-old boy. A sickening feeling started in the pit of her stomach. Outside the glass, a narrow catwalk encircled the tower; but crouched beside the light, Hazel couldn't see it all. She forced her trembling legs to stand. What she saw made her close her eyes instantly. But when she opened them again nothing had changed. She hadn't imagined it. This wasn't a dream. This was real.

Ned was outside on the catwalk, on the far side of the tower. At least, Ned's *upper* body was on the catwalk, and he was gripping the iron railing that encircled it as if his life depended on it. And from what Hazel could tell, it did.

Hazel desperately needed to throw up. She could see now what had happened. The wooden floor of the catwalk had rotted and Ned had broken through. She could see the splintered edges of the planks behind him, jutting into thin air. That must have been the sound she'd heard as she came up the stairs.

Her little brother was dangling from a railing hundreds of feet in the air, with nothing but rocks below. And there was no one to help, no one to save him. Only Hazel, a girl so terrified of heights she couldn't move.

CHAPTER FOURTEEN

Black spots swam before Hazel's eyes and the sound of the wind died away, replaced by a faint buzzing in her ears. Hazel remembered how she felt right before she'd fainted in the underground passage. Exactly like this. Cold sweat covered her skin. Her body swayed.

"Hazel?" Ned's voice was thin and taut, like a rubber band stretched almost to the point of snapping. "Don't faint, okay? Hazel? *Help!*"

Hazel took a deep breath. If she thought about it, she wouldn't be able to do it. She forced herself through the open hatch that led to the catwalk outside. This platform was far narrower than the one in the library and there were treacherous gaps in the railing to Hazel's right. It would be the easiest thing in the world to slip through one of those openings and plummet to her death. But the gaps weren't her biggest fear. Ned, presumably, hadn't known those boards were rotten until they gave way. If parts of the platform couldn't support Ned's smaller, lighter body, Hazel couldn't be sure that the flooring between her and Ned would support *her.*

All she could do was hope.

Hazel crawled forward on hands and knees, her left side brushing against the tower. Ned was only a few feet away now, facing her. His face was contorted with fear and the effort of holding onto the railing; he was almost unrecognizable. Hazel paused. When someone falls through ice on a pond, aren't you supposed to squirm forward on your belly until you can throw them a rope? She had no rope. And no time. Ned's eyes were closed now and his lips were moving. Was he praying? Out of the corner of her eye Hazel saw a tiny movement.

Ned's hand was slipping.

She sprang forward. It was kind of like diving for a loose ball— *if* you were diving for that ball on a rickety piece of platform a thousand miles up in the air instead of on a nice solid court.

And *if* the loose ball wasn't a ball at all, but the most precious person in the world.

She landed on her stomach with a *thud* that rattled the boards, but the planks didn't give way. Grabbing Ned's shoulders, Hazel heaved with every fibre of every muscle she possessed. Lifting and pulling a dead weight when you're on your stomach isn't easy. And no matter how many times Hazel tried to demonstrate later just how she had plucked her brother from the jaws of certain death, she was never able to do it again.

But she only had to do it once.

It happened so fast. The broken floorboards caught on the front of Ned's jacket as she yanked, ripping the fabric into ribbons. But before Hazel even had time to register the sound, Ned was lying half beside her and half on top of her, and they were both breathing hard and crying and laughing all at once. It was several moments before either one of them could move, but when they did, they bolted for the hatch and hurtled down the staircase to the room below the light in record time. Then they sat on the floor and just stared at each other for several minutes.

Ned was the first to speak.

"So. No clue."

With shaking hands, he removed his spectacles from his nose and began polishing them with his sleeve. Hazel felt a rush of tears again and swallowed hard to avoid losing it completely. She was glad that Ned hadn't said anything mushy like *Thank you for saving my life,* or told her how much he loved her. She couldn't have handled that, not right now. She closed her eyes and took two deep, steadying breaths, the way she always did to calm herself at the free throw line. When Hazel opened her eyes she managed a smile.

"Gee, if only someone could have told you the clue wasn't going to be up there."

Ned gave her a watery grin. He started to get up but winced and put a hand on his side.

"Uh-oh," Hazel said. "What now—bruise? Cut? Broken rib?"

Ned lifted his torn jacket and sweater to reveal a half-dozen jagged tears across his midriff, just starting to ooze droplets of blood.

"That's nasty," Hazel said. "Not deep but long. A scrape like that—we better get you home."

Ned grimaced. "Could we *not* tell them how it happened?"

For a second Hazel was tempted, but she shook her head. "Uncle Seamus needs to know about all the damage to the lighthouse. Not just what the storm did to the cottage but also the rotten planks on the tower. We can't risk someone else getting hurt."

"I guess. They're not going to be happy."

"No."

Slowly, painfully, they made their way downstairs. They trudged through the ruins of the cottage to collect their things, lost in thought. Hazel tucked the old newspapers inside her backpack. She glanced at her watch.

"Hey, Ned, it's getting late. At least one of the twins is probably home right now. We're both tired and you're hurt. Maybe we should call them and let them know where we are?"

"Yeah. We'd better warn 'em that it'll take us a while to get home," Ned said. "At least the wind's died down, though."

It was true. The wind had disappeared, leaving the afternoon calm and sunny. That was something. The walk home would be long but it would be easier than the walk to the lighthouse.

"I'll call," Hazel said, pulling her cell phone from the pocket of the jacket she'd borrowed from Deirdre. "If Matt's going to yell at anyone it should be me. I'm the oldest."

Matt picked up on the second ring. He didn't yell, although there was a long, ominous silence after Hazel described where they were. Hazel found herself gabbling to fill the void. She decided not to mention Ned's near-death experience over the phone. She just said they were both tired and Ned had a bad scrape and they might be a while getting home. She was about to ask if Matt was still there, when he erupted in exasperation.

"For Pete's sake, you . . . you *kids*. If you wanted to go see the lighthouse, why didn't you wait until I could take you? It would have been a lot easier and safer."

"We didn't have any trouble finding the place," Hazel began, but Matt didn't let her finish.

"But you didn't have to hike all that way. I would have brought you in the boat. There's a perfectly safe passage through the rocks on the north side of the inlet, and a little stretch of sand where we pull the boat up."

"Oh." Hazel couldn't think of anything else to say.

Matt gave a long-suffering sigh. "Never mind. I'll be there in half an hour. Just sit tight and don't move."

Hazel flipped the phone closed and put it back in her pocket. So the whole long trek to the lighthouse had been a complete waste. Now she was so tired her bones ached and Ned had almost been killed and all they had to look forward to was everyone freaking as soon as they saw the scrapes on Ned's chest.

Ned handed Hazel a ginger cookie and took one for himself. They sat on the rocks and munched and listened to the gulls.

"It couldn't have been this lighthouse anyway. It doesn't fit the clue," Ned said finally.

"What?"

He pulled the crumpled sheet of paper from his back pocket and pointed to the line that read: "A beacon of light that was never extinguished."

"Dad would know this light hasn't been operational for decades. Charlotte too."

Hazel's shoulders slumped. "We almost got you killed and we're no further along in solving the mystery. Some detectives we'd make."

"Yup." Ned chewed thoughtfully. "Although, you do have your nice little collection of old newspapers. And we're getting to have a picnic by the water. So, not a total loss."

"You're getting loopy from loss of blood or something."

Matt's expression when he arrived was grim. It grew grimmer after he saw the ruined cottage, and changed to furious once he saw Ned's cuts and scrapes. By the time Hazel was explaining how Ned got them, Matt's face was a thunderstorm waiting to break. Hazel actually heard him count to ten before he spoke. But when he did, it sounded as if he was talking to himself.

"Okay, first we'll have to post warning signs, but then we'll have to get someone out here to start on repairs. Tourist season's over but you never know with lighthouse nuts . . . Before we go I'll see if I can rig up something to let any trespassers know they're putting their lives at risk."

"We'll help." Hazel stepped forward, but Matt stopped her with a hand on her shoulder.

"No chance. You two have done enough for one day. Sit."

As Matt disappeared around the corner of the cottage, Ned frowned.

"You'd never know he's seventeen, would you. I think he was born forty. Maybe fifty."

Fifteen minutes later, Matt was helping Hazel and Ned into the shallow metal boat, having roped off the entrance to the tower and fastened handwritten signs that said NO TRESPASSING and DANGER to the doors of both the tower and the cottage. As the Boston Whaler thumped across the shining water, Hazel shivered, but she was grateful for the wind. It made conversation difficult.

Ned, on the other hand, never knew when to leave well enough alone.

"So, Matt, are there any other lighthouses around here?"

"What?" Matt didn't take his hand off the tiller but he stared at Ned with a look that made Hazel glad Ned's life jacket was securely fastened.

"Don't worry, I'm all done exploring lighthouses . . . for now, anyway. I just wondered if there were anymore. With lights that still work."

Matt muttered something under his breath. Hazel was pretty sure she didn't want to know what it was. Then he gave another martyred sigh.

"Our light was decommissioned back in the 1970s. They put up a floating light farther out in the lake. There's another lighthouse around the north side of the island—it's still running. Don't get any ideas, though. It's government owned and operated and they don't allow visitors."

Ned fell silent, and Hazel hoped he'd stay that way. But as they rounded the last bay, he tried again. "What about the harbour? Isn't there a lighthouse near the marina?"

"Sure, but it's not real, it's just for show." Matt steered the boat toward the castle boathouse. He cut the motor and the whaler drifted perfectly into place. Matt hopped onto the wooden walkway and secured the boat, knotting the ropes with the ease of someone who'd done it so many times he didn't have to think about what he was doing. As she watched, Hazel decided she'd ask Matt to teach her some of those knots. Matt glanced up as if feeling her eyes on him. Hazel gulped. She'd wait until he was in a better mood. Like next summer.

"With everything that's going on with Charlotte, I can't believe you guys would do something so . . ." Matt focused on Hazel. "And you—you're the oldest! I thought you had more sense."

Matt stomped ahead of them toward the castle and what Hazel was sure would be a mortifying telephone call to Uncle Seamus.

"Maybe it's a *painting* of a lighthouse?" Ned said, as if Matt hadn't spoken. "Or maybe there's a lighthouse statue somewhere around here?"

Hazel cuffed him lightly on the head as they followed Matt inside.

Deirdre and Oliver listened wide-eyed to the story, while Matt dialled Uncle Seamus. To his credit, Ned insisted on picking up the extension and trying to take the blame for climbing the tower. But when Matt handed his phone to Hazel, even without scolding, Uncle Seamus managed to make them both feel bad.

"I had no idea the lighthouse had suffered such damage and that is my fault entirely." Uncle Seamus's voice was heavy with regret. "You were imprudent, Ned, but the blame is mine. The lighthouse and cottage are my responsibility and so are you. I'm grateful I don't have to contact your father with news of your untimely demise."

"So you're not going to punish us?" Ned asked.

Hazel winced. It didn't take a genius to know that you should never mention punishment if an adult hadn't already brought it up.

"Ah, yes . . . punishment." Uncle Seamus sounded like he was chewing on a pencil. "Well, er, Matt will supervise the cleaning and disinfecting of your wounds, Ned, and that of course is hardly painless . . . punishment enough, one might say. But of course there must be some further penance . . . ah yes! You are both grounded!"

He made the last announcement with the triumphant air of a magician producing a rabbit. Hazel had to act fast, before Ned opened his mouth again.

"Oh, grounded. Yikes. Like, um, for a whole day?" she said in a downcast voice.

Uncle Seamus paused. "*Two* whole days," he said firmly. "That should show Deirdre—I mean, *all* of you children—just how seriously I take your safety."

Hazel grinned. Sometimes she thought Uncle Seamus feared only one person—his daughter.

"Okay," Ned said. "We promise we won't leave the castle grounds for two days."

"And of course the treasure hunt should be cancelled immediately. Now, put Matt on again, please. I want an update on Charlotte's condition." Uncle Seamus sounded like a man who had already moved on to other things. Hazel could hear papers rustling in the background.

"Say what?" Ned sputtered into the phone.

"I don't have time to discuss this with you, Ned—put Matthew on *now*."

Apparently Charlotte had regained consciousness and was out of danger. Hazel saw Ned brush an arm across his face. She had the same tears of relief in her eyes, although she couldn't help a brief flicker of resentment toward Matt for not telling them sooner. But listening to the teenager assure Uncle Seamus that he didn't need to cut short his business trip, Hazel felt a pang of guilt. Matt was always the responsible one. Between adjusting to university, and coping with Charlotte in hospital, the last thing he needed to worry about was Hazel and Ned and what death trap they'd explore next. Maybe Uncle Seamus was right to end the treasure hunt.

She was relieved when Matt departed for the hospital, sending Mark home to make dinner. The lanky twin made them all laugh as he described the crazy stories he'd fed Charlotte after she came to.

"You didn't really tell her she'd hurt her head in a water-skiing competition?" Oliver said.

"Well, of course I said she wore a wetsuit because of the cold. But I don't think she believed me." Mark looked thoughtful. "I may have gone over the top when I said she was part of a human pyramid."

"So she really doesn't remember anything since Thanksgiving?" Deirdre said. "Is that, like, just for now? Or will she remember later?"

Mark shrugged. He tossed a handful of chopped carrots and onions into the pot of stew bubbling on the stove, then turned to face Hazel and Ned, his expression confused.

"So what's all this I hear about you two hanging out at The Lighthouse Tavern?"

Ned raised an eyebrow.

"We didn't go to any tavern, we went to the lighthouse—the one along the shore."

Mark's expression cleared. "Oh. Well, *that* makes more sense. I didn't stop to figure out what Matt was grumbling about; the nurses at the hospital were fussing about how only one of us could be in Charlotte's room at a time. But I thought he said you'd been hanging out at The Lighthouse."

"What's The Lighthouse?" Hazel asked.

"One of the oldest continuously operating inns in North America, according to the owners. You can't stay there any-more—it's just a pub now. But it's got this little carved light-house over the door, with a gaslight inside. Legend has it the light's never gone out."

A pub? The sort of place that might serve sandwiches? Hazel and Ned looked at each other.

"It's an okay place," Oliver said. "One of my friends owns it. Her parents own it, I mean. We go there for lunch sometimes; it's not far from school."

"But enough about that," Mark said. "Why's my brother so cranky about you guys visiting *our* lighthouse?"

Deirdre and Oliver had already heard the tale, and they joined in the retelling. Hazel wished they could just forget the whole thing. She tried to downplay the drama, but when Mark saw the bandages on Ned's chest, he gave a theatrical shudder.

"Do me a favour, bro? Take it easy with this treasure hunt. We don't need another man down right now."

Hazel and Ned exchanged glances. Uncle Seamus obviously hadn't told anyone he was stopping the treasure hunt!

"They'll have to take it easy for a couple of days anyway," Deirdre said. "They're grounded."

"Sis, you may think you're the boss of this house—" Mark began, but Hazel interrupted.

"No, we really are. Uncle Seamus said so."

Mark's reply was cut off by the ringing of the phone. He answered and his expression changed as he listened.

"I see . . . okay . . . We'll see you soon—drive safely." Mark replaced the phone carefully and turned to face the others, looking sombre.

"That was Matt. We'd better hope Charlotte gets her memory back soon. The police came to interview her; they're sure now that she was attacked. They found a big stick in the stable that somebody used to knock her out. It's covered in blood."

CHAPTER FIFTEEN

Hazel was back in the strange, windowless room—only this time it wasn't empty. Everywhere she turned she saw jewels, dazzling emeralds, sea-blue sapphires and glowing rubies, all heaped in piles like candies in a dish. Hazel wanted to touch them but they melted away, and suddenly the cruel woman from the painting in Clive Pritchard's shop appeared, hissing at her: *Thief! Give me back my ring.*

Hazel turned to run and saw Mercy Frump, crying again: *What has he done?* And then Mercy changed into Charlotte. There was someone behind her. Hazel tried to scream a warning, but when she opened her mouth no sound came.

"Hazel? You awake? It's me, Oliver." There was a quiet tap on her door. "Can I come in?"

Hazel rolled over and looked at the clock on her desk. It was 6:30 in the morning—much too early to get up. But if she tried to go back to sleep she'd probably have another nightmare.

"Uh, sure."

Oliver slid into the room as if fearful he'd been followed.

"I already talked about this with Ned, and he said yes, but he said I should check with you first."

"About what?" Hazel yawned, looking around for her sweatshirt.

"It's obvious you guys are supposed to be looking for something at The Lighthouse Tavern. I could tell from your faces when Mark was talking at dinner. Since you're grounded, I'm volunteering to go get the clue."

"Seriously? But, Oliver—" Hazel began.

Oliver didn't let her finish. "Lyla's always asking me to come over to the tavern for lunch. It's a nice place. I don't know why your dad said that stuff about the hospitality and the sandwiches—the food there is great! And if I forget my lunch on the bus today, I'll have the perfect excuse."

Hazel knew this was the moment to come clean and tell Oliver the treasure hunt had been cancelled. Instead, she found herself saying, "You don't even know what you're looking for—or where to look."

Oliver considered this. "You didn't ask; I offered. And Ned just said to check under the doormat, if there is one, and bring back whatever I find."

"Oh. Well, thanks, Oliver. It's nice of you to help out." Hazel was amazed at how calm she sounded. She was disobeying Uncle Seamus, and using little Oliver to do it!

Oliver beamed. Then a shadow seemed to pass across his face.

"Of course you realize I'm taking a big risk."

"Why?" Guilt curdled in Hazel's stomach. Did he know, after all? Or did he just suspect?

"If I leave my lunch on the bus and Lyla doesn't come to school today, I'll starve!"

Hazel laughed in relief and swatted him away. After Oliver had gone, she flopped back on the pillows and contemplated the day ahead. She and Ned were grounded, so they wouldn't leave the castle. Atta girl, Hazel, she told herself, break no more than one rule a day. But there was still a lot they could do. It was time to focus on what Ned called the "ancient mystery": the spell book, the jewels, the diary . . . and maybe even her dreams. It was time to find out just what secrets Land's End was guarding.

Once Deirdre and Oliver had left for school, and Matt had headed off to divide his day between the hospital and the university, Mark announced that he planned to devote most of his time to studying in his room. This made Ned happy, because there was an excellent chance Mark would take a break at some point to make cookies or crepes or some kind of treat. It made Hazel happy because it meant the teenager would be around if they needed him, but out of the way while she and Ned researched the mystery.

They decided to work in Hazel's room for now—the jewels, diary and spell book were there, along with the sketches, and several armfuls of books on life in the nineteenth century, which had gradually made their way from the library.

"We did the right thing, you know," Ned said, as he snagged the comfiest chair. "I mean, letting Oliver go look for the lighthouse clue."

"I hope so." Hazel picked up a dull-looking book on life in Upper Canada. "I hate disobeying Uncle Seamus but I can't stand the thought of abandoning the treasure hunt now. I feel as if it's important somehow—as if we *have* to keep going."

"Me too," Ned declared.

The book was as boring as Hazel had suspected. After a few minutes, she set it down and turned to a history of magic that she'd found in the library. Maybe it would help her make sense of the spell book.

People seemed to have believed in magic and witchcraft for centuries, but not in a happy way. It was generally feared and reviled, and anyone accused of practising it was given a rough time.

"You know, if I had a spell book, I'd hide it too," Hazel said after a while. "Depending on when you lived, if people thought you were a witch they did everything from shun you to kill you."

"Mmmm," Ned muttered, his head bent over the spell book.

A few pages later, the drawing of a mouse caught Hazel's eye. The chapter was titled "Familiars—Domestic and Divining." Hazel didn't know what a "familiar" was, but she could feel her heart race as she read further.

According to the book, witches were sometimes said to use animals to work their magic. A sign of a witch could be the presence of a small, domestic animal such as a cat, dog or even a mouse, living in the witch's home, tame and even trained.

"So what? How is that different from having a pet?" Hazel murmured.

"What?" Ned glanced up from the book of spells.

"Nothing." Hazel shook her head. "At least, nothing yet."

Domestic animals were used by witches to cast curses, the book said. To divine the future, or tell prophecies, a witch needed the help of a larger wild animal like a deer, or in some cases, a wild bird—such as an owl or hawk.

Hazel closed the book with a *thump*. She didn't believe in magic; she absolutely didn't believe in magic. This was crazy.

Ned looked up at the sound. "You know something, Hazel? I didn't pay enough attention to this book before. But some of these spells might just work."

Hazel sat up straighter. "Ned! You're not trying to tell me *you* believe in magic? Mr. Science? You believe in potions and incantations?"

"Not incantations, no. But the incantations and nutty stuff, they're mostly in the second half of the book. The first half has a lot of what I'd call first aid. Homeopathic stuff."

"Romeo what?"

Ned frowned. "Now you're just being silly. Homeopathy. Like folk remedies, sort of. I mean some of it's silly and superstitious, but a lot of it makes sense."

"Would any of it actually help someone who was sick?"

"Sure." Ned nodded. "Sick or injured. In the old days people didn't have doctors nearby all the time and anyway medicine wasn't always that good. People had to handle a lot of stuff on their own. Like mix up oatmeal poultices and salves. You know, to make a burn feel better or help a chest cold."

"How come you know so much about it?" Hazel looked at her brother with suspicion. "Is your chemistry club getting carried away again?"

Ned peered at Hazel over the top of his spectacles. "I never do anything that people would have to eat. I mean, sure, when I was younger I was working on a way to induce twelve-hour hiccups, but I gave up that kind of thing a long time ago. I didn't want to poison someone accidentally."

"Thank goodness."

"Anyway, lots of the 'spells' in the first part of the book are based on plants. Herbs or wildflowers. That makes sense because lots of drugs we buy today are based on plants. Pharmaceutical companies figure out what chemicals in the plant are useful and then they synthesize the plant DNA—"

"Stop!" Hazel put her hands over her ears and glared at Ned. "Too much info. What does this have to do with anything?"

"I'm just saying that the first part of the spell book has a lot of stuff in it that amounts to sensible home remedies if you ignore all the fancy magic words."

"And the second half of the book?"

"It's garbage." Ned thrust the book across the desk. "See for yourself."

Hazel flipped slowly through the pages. The whole book

looked silly to her, although the spells nearer the end of the book definitely had a more sinister tone. Blood kept showing up as a key ingredient, for one thing—the blood of birds and animals. And it seemed to be important to do lots of stuff at night or under cover of darkness.

"Hey, Ned, did you notice that the handwriting changes too?"

Ned nodded. "Yeah, I wondered about that. But I figure my handwriting changes all the time. Like when I'm in a hurry, or when I switch pens."

Hazel flipped through a few more pages. "Yeah, mine changes too. I look at stuff I wrote last year and I can't believe how different it looks. But isn't that just because we're still kids? Anyway, it's not like the writing in the magic book changes from day to day. It's like what you said about the spells—the first half looks different from the second."

Hazel handed the book back to Ned. "So, what if it's not the same book? I mean, what if two people wrote it?"

Ned looked thoughtful. "Like maybe the first writer was sort of normal but then a crazy dude got hold of the book and started scribbling."

Hazel sat very still, silently replaying her nightmare from that morning.

"Yes. Ned, what if the first writer was Mercy. You know, a normal, nice person, maybe a little shy, just like Diary Guy said."

Ned jumped out of the chair and began pacing around the room. "Sure! She could have been interested in plants and heal-ing. I'll bet she didn't even call it a book of spells & magicks. That was Crazy Dude. He stole her book and started writing all that weird stuff."

"Crazy Dude? Try Edwin Frump!" Hazel said. "He was just as

creepy as his portrait. He was spying on Diary Guy and taking his stuff and blaming his sister. It has to have been him. Oh!"

Hazel looked at Ned. She felt incredibly stupid and incredibly brilliant all at the same time.

"The stuff, Ned. The stuff that went missing from Diary Guy's room!"

"What about it?"

"It's all there, in the book." Hazel couldn't sit still anymore either. She hopped up off the bed and thrust the magic book into Ned's hands. "You read all the charms and potions, and you paid more attention to the ingredients than I did. Check—check the freaky spells in the back half of the book. See if any of them use a lock of human hair, or a shoelace. Or nail clippings!"

Ned turned the pages with care. He began to jot notes on a sheet of paper. After a few minutes he picked up the diary and began leafing through it, stopping every few pages to write something or glance between the diary and the magic book. Hazel wanted to read over his shoulder but she knew that would make Ned cranky and lead to an argument and she just wanted to get the answers as quickly as possible.

Instead, Hazel paced. She knew she was right, she just knew it. Edwin Cornelius Frump was a witch! Or a wannabe.

"Done." After what seemed an eternity, Ned closed the books and put down the pen. With an air of solemnity, he handed Hazel the sheet of paper on which he'd made notes. Then he removed his glasses and rubbed his eyes wearily. "This is deeply weird."

Hazel could only nod. Ned's notes consisted of two columns. Down the left-hand side of the page he'd listed the items stolen from Diary Guy. Down the right-hand side Ned had named the spell or magic potion that included that item as an ingredient. It looked like this:

Shoelace   spell for binding

Watch chain   spell for releasing

Lock of hair   spell for blinding
                     spell to restore sight
                     spell for causing hiccups
                     spell for curing hiccups

Nail clippings   spell for forgetfulness/amnesia
                     spell for causing stomach ache
                     spell for curing stomach ache

Handwriting   spell for changing someone's mind

"Did you notice the hiccups?" Ned's voice suddenly sounded much younger. "And I'm named after this guy. It's creepy."

Hazel set the sheet of paper down on the desk. "You're nothing like him, Ned. I was teasing before. So what if you have the same name? And so what if you share an interest in hiccups. Lots of people are interested in hiccups."

Ned grimaced. Hazel started to laugh. "Okay, maybe not *lots* of people, but it's just hiccups, Ned. Pretty tame. You're not going around trying to blind people, for goodness' sake. Or bind people. Which was it?"

"Both. Well, he was *trying* to do both." Ned gave a contemptuous sneer, and for a moment Hazel really was reminded of the portrait. "Obviously his spells are ridiculous, and there's no way they'd work."

"Obviously." Hazel glanced at the paper again. "Um, what exactly does 'binding' mean? Tying someone up?"

Ned sighed. "Kind of. The binding spell sounds like it's meant to be the opposite of the releasing spell. Kind of like a psychic kidnapping—you make it so the person can't bring themselves to walk out your door, no matter how much they want to."

"Nasty."

"Yeah." Ned shook his head. "That pretty much sums up dear great-great-great-great-whatever-he-is Edwin."

"I was just reading this book on the history of magic," Hazel said, thinking aloud. "People with pets were sometimes suspected of being witches—they thought cats and mice could be used to cast spells. There's a mouse in that portrait of Edwin. I thought that was an odd thing for the painter to include . . . I guess it could have been a pet."

Hazel plopped back down on her bed. Ned flung himself down on the window seat. For several minutes they just lay there, staring at the ceiling, lost in thought. Then Ned rolled over on his side and looked at Hazel.

"I need a break. This is too dark and kind of disturbing. How about we go shoot hoops?"

An hour or so of dribbling and shooting worked wonders. Before Hazel's best friend, Alysha, had moved to Paris, it was what they'd always done to clear their minds and take a break from homework or household chores. Alysha called it "getting the cobwebs out." Now, with Ned as a partner to run drills, Hazel could feel herself relaxing. It was as if they were forcing the grip of Edwin Frump to loosen. Her strange dreams receded into the background, and Hazel found herself smiling as Ned attempted to cut past her. The late October air was crisp and fresh, and once they'd warmed up, it felt like the perfect temperature.

Ned was so much shorter than her, it wasn't a fair match-up, but he was quick and several times he managed to beat her off the dribble. It felt like forever since Hazel had truly played. She was rusty, that was for sure, but the longer they practised, the more Hazel imagined she could feel the rust flaking away.

By the time Mark summoned them for lunch, Hazel knew that Ned's spirits had risen along with hers. And once their bellies were filled with piping hot soup and far too many of Mark's mouth-watering biscuits, she felt ready to tackle the mystery again. But Mark had other plans.

"Listen, I studied so hard this morning I definitely earned an afternoon off. I plan to spend it cooking and baking—but I want your help."

"Seriously?" Ned looked at Hazel. She shrugged.

"Of course, technically I don't need your help," Mark said. "But consider it good PR for you. I want to make a bunch of stuff that Matt can take to Charlotte tonight. Hospital food being . . . well, not really anything a normal human being would recognize as food. And if you two served as my sous-chefs it might win you points with my grumpy twin."

The job of a sous-chef, they soon learned, consisted largely of fetching and measuring ingredients for Mark, chopping nuts, vegetables or fruit, and occasionally stirring something or watching to make sure it didn't burn or boil. It was fun, and Mark allowed plenty of sampling. But after a few hours Hazel was relieved when the phone rang and it was Frankie.

"I just wanted to let you know that Sketchbook came through! I found out something about your jewels."

Hazel turned her back on Mark and Ned, but they seemed more interested in whether the brownies were ready to come out of the oven. Keeping her voice low, Hazel said, "That's great. This isn't a good time, though—can you send me an e-mail?"

"I've been trying, but I'm having some problems. I think my computer picked up a virus. It may take a while to get it sorted out, and I thought you might be in a hurry."

"I see." Hazel grabbed a pencil and a piece of paper to take notes. "Okay, go ahead."

Frankie's contacts on the Sketchbook network had been intrigued by the photographs of the jewels. Several people had forwarded them to friends or acquaintances in museums and antiques shops, and some of those people had forwarded them as well. The jewels were most likely real, and from the settings, looked as if they dated from the mid to late 1800s. The ring was said to be particularly rare and valuable, and already someone was angling to buy it.

"I don't imagine your family will want to part with any of the jewels," Frankie said. "But this woman says she's a jewellery expert and museum consultant, and she represents some billionaire who's been looking for a ring exactly like yours for years. Some sort of long-lost family heirloom, apparently. She didn't give the billionaire's name, but her name is Vera—Vera Thirdcclip. With two 'c's.'"

No sooner had Frankie hung up than Deirdre and Oliver arrived, accompanied by Matt.

"Ooh, it's our lucky day," Deirdre said, inhaling the aromas. "We get a lift from Matt *and* brownies."

"Hands off, these are for Charlotte's nurses!" Mark made a shooing motion at his sister, then grinned at his twin. "Hazel and Ned have been slaving over a hot stove all afternoon."

Matt nodded. "I'm just home to grab the food. I'll drop it at the hospital on my way back to campus—there's a lecture this evening I don't want to miss."

Oliver slung his jacket onto a peg by the door and failed to notice it slip to the floor. He stepped unconcernedly over it.

"Hey, Ned, what's new?"

Hazel stifled a grin at the studiously casual look on Oliver's face as he slapped palms with her brother, skilfully passing a tiny envelope to Ned in the process.

Mark had already put most of the food in containers.

Now he took the first load out to the car. Matt followed, carefully balancing a tureen of soup, a bowl of salad and a plate of brownies. He paused on the threshold.

"Thanks for doing this. I know Charlotte will appreciate it, even if most of this food gets eaten by hospital staff. I'll be back by 11 p.m. Don't burn the house down while I'm gone."

"Okay, we'll wait 'til you get back," Oliver said (but only after the door had closed behind Matt).

"I'll be back in a second," Hazel said, gathering up the papers she'd used to take notes during her phone call with Frankie. "I just want to take this stuff up to my room."

As she climbed the stairs, Hazel found herself wondering about the anonymous billionaire who'd been searching for a ring like theirs. Exactly like theirs? Somehow she'd imagined their ring was unique . . . although, of course there was that painting of the nasty-looking woman in Clive Pritchard's shop. Her ring sure looked like theirs too.

Hazel paused on the threshold. What exactly *were* the odds of three identical ruby rings being made back in Victorian times, one for the Frumps, one for the mysterious woman in Pritchard's shop, and one for the guy who'd hired Vera What's-her-name?

Darting to her desk, Hazel grabbed a pencil and stared at the name she'd jotted down from Frankie: *Vera Thirdcclip*. What kind of a name was that? With trembling fingers, she wrote another name beneath it: *Clive Pritchard*. She counted aloud; each name had fourteen letters. Then, slowly, deliberately, Hazel drew a line through the letters that appeared in both names. It was a perfect match: *Vera Thirdcclip* was an anagram for *Clive Pritchard*.

CHAPTER SIXTEEN

It had to be a coincidence. Even if it wasn't, Hazel needed to decide it was a coincidence, close her eyes and get some sleep. But as the hours ticked by and sleep refused to come, Hazel became more and more convinced that there was no such thing as coincidence.

The rest of the evening had passed in a blur, with Hazel desperate to escape to her room so she could think. Clive Pritchard had a thing for anagrams, she knew. He scrambled the letters of his own name to make aliases for himself and his accomplices. And when Pritchard invented a fake artist from the Romantic period, so he could sell counterfeit art, he used the letters from his partner's name to create the artist's identity.

But Clive Pritchard was behind bars. And Hazel was NOT going to worry Ned or anyone else with something that just had to be a coincidence.

When she finally drifted off, it was an uneasy, restless sleep. And when she awoke, everything felt wrong. Her muscles were stiff and her brain felt sluggish, cluttered by bits of dreams that clung like stubborn cobwebs. Hazel had a vague memory of seeing Edwin Frump sneak into Ned's room while he slept. And Mercy, writing a clue while sitting at Hazel's desk, but the ink coming out of her pen was blood-red. It had stained her hands. And Diary Guy—there had been something about him, too, selling paintings in Clive Pritchard's shop? It was all mixed up. Images flitted through Hazel's brain, but when she reached for them they vanished.

It was annoying, then, to trudge down to breakfast only to find everyone else already finishing the meal and obnoxiously cheerful.

"Looks like the last couple of days are catching up with you," Matt observed, as Hazel slumped into her chair. "Just as well you're still grounded—it might force you to take things easy for once."

"Uh-huh."

"It's a good thing you're not grounded tomorrow, though." Deirdre put Oliver's lunch into his backpack and grabbed her jacket. "You haven't forgotten about the big Halloween party at the pioneer village, have you?"

"Halloween is tomorrow night?" Hazel couldn't believe how quickly time had passed. She could feel her resolve stiffening. They'd be heading back to school soon. Well to heck with crazy Edwin and Clive Pritchard, and even Uncle Seamus. No way was she going back until she'd solved everything: the historical mystery *and* the treasure hunt too!

"Do we need to get costumes?" Ned cleared away his cereal bowl and poured himself a glass of juice. Then he slid the glass over to Hazel and poured another for himself. "You don't look so good, Hazel. You okay?"

Hazel shook her head glumly. "Bad dreams."

"Harsh," Deirdre said. She already had her jacket on and was hustling Oliver into his. "I hate nightmares. Sometimes it helps to talk about them—you realize how silly they are. I'd stay and listen but Oliver and I are getting a lift to school with Mimi—oh, there she is!"

"I'm off as well." Matt grabbed an apple from the counter. "I've got a meeting with a tutorial assistant and then I'm going to check on Charlotte. I'll probably pick up Deirdre and Oliver on my way home. We can figure out costumes tonight. Be good!"

As the kitchen door slammed, Hazel laid her head on the table and let out a long sigh. "Why did everyone else in this house get a decent sleep except me? It's not fair! I'm too tired to think and we have so much to think about."

From an armchair by the fireplace, Mark wearily raised his coffee cup in greeting.

"You're not the only one who didn't sleep well, cousin. I stayed up way too late hitting the books." Mark stifled a yawn. "Come to think of it, I may just mosey on back to bed for a few hours. Catch you later."

"I've got the sixth clue, but I think you should eat something before you look at it again," Ned advised. "You always feel better after you eat. And I do mean *you*."

Hazel had been so distracted the night before by the anagram that she hadn't been able to focus on the clue Oliver had found. Now, munching on toast, she read it over again with bleary eyes. But it didn't seem any clearer.

Where the boat goes,
Near the river and the rose,
Inside an old flue,
There sits the last clue.
You risk a grim fate,
If you come too late.

Ned made a face. "The last lines are sort of . . . mean."

156

He had a point. It wasn't like their father to threaten them.

"Maybe Charlotte wrote this one?" Hazel sighed. "I guess we need to find a river and a boat. What do you suppose 'inside an old flue' means?"

"He didn't even spell it right." Ned frowned. "How can you get inside a flu? Like, inside the nose of someone who's sick? Talk about gross. Maybe Dad means inside a test tube filled with the flu virus. But it's an *old* flu . . ."

Ned seemed to have forgotten Hazel's presence. He kept talking, his excitement growing, but she knew he was speaking to himself.

"There could be a top-secret lab around here where scientists keep old viruses to study. Security on a place like that's gotta be tight. I'll have to hack my way in . . ."

This was a genius at work? Hazel reached forward and snapped her fingers under his nose.

"Ned! It's an old *flue.* As in a chimney? As in Santa Claus?"

"Oh." Ned blinked, and Hazel could see his disappointment. "Right."

"Listen, I need to have a shower and get dressed. Meet me in the library in half an hour? I have an idea about where we can look next, since we're not supposed to leave Land's End."

"Should I bring the laptop?"

"Yeah, bring the laptop. In fact, let's bring everything—the clues, the diary, the spell book, the jewels. And maybe even those old newspapers, the ones I found at the lighthouse. You never know."

Ned headed to the door. "What about Mark?"

"A teenage boy who was up all night studying?" Hazel grinned. "I don't think we have to worry about him for hours."

Still, when Hazel arrived at the library, scrubbed and dressed, Ned insisted on keeping the jewels hidden beneath his sweater.

Everything else he had spread out on one of the long library tables. Anything connected to the historical mystery Ned had placed at one end of the table. The treasure hunt clues were laid out in order, one through seven, at the other end. Oliver's laptop sat in the middle.

"Good." Hazel surveyed the evidence table. "Now, where did I see those maps?"

In a few minutes they had a pile of map books and drawings, painstaking and wildly inaccurate depictions of the New World from hundreds of years ago. They proved a great distraction for Hazel, with their claims that monsters inhabited the waters north of Newfoundland. But she abandoned them when Ned found an enormous volume called *Views of Île du Loup* and dragged it over to the table. A big cloud of dust rose into the air when he dropped it beside the laptop.

"Careful—that's probably valuable," Hazel said.

"I think I hurt myself more than the book." Ned winced, pressing a hand against his stomach.

"Your scrapes?"

Ned nodded. But after a moment, his face cleared.

"It's okay now. So what are we looking for, exactly?"

"The first few clues were inside the castle. Then we got to explore the grounds, with that clue in the garden and another inside the chapel. Then the clues started taking us into the village." Hazel carefully turned the pages of the map book until she reached a drawing of Ville St-Pierre. "There. Now let's see if we can find a river."

"That's your great idea?" Ned made a face. "Hazel, these maps are old. They're out of date. Things change."

"Not everything. Rivers don't."

"Uh, have your teachers mentioned this little thing called global warming? Climate change? Erosion?"

But Hazel pointed to the map. A thin ribbon of silver started in a forested area inland and wound down around the out-skirts of the village, emptying eventually into the lake at a point about halfway between Land's End and the village. It was labelled *Rose River.*

"Huh." Ned was silent for a moment. "Okay, but I bet we could have found it faster on the Internet."

Hazel stared at the map. The Rose River sounded familiar somehow, but she couldn't place it. Maybe it would come to her if she stopped trying. Hazel began leafing through the old maps and was soon engrossed in Frontenac as it must have looked more than a hundred years ago. But Ned couldn't sit still. He paced the length of the room, grumbling.

"Who does Dad think he is, anyway? And what's all this about a grim fate if we don't get there in time? We're thinking as fast as we can. Plus, we're grounded. It's not like we could rush right out there and grab the clue today even if we knew where to look."

Ned threw himself down into a chair at the far end of the table from the clues. He fingered the diary and spell book, before moving on to the pile of old newspapers from the light-house. Soon he, too, was lost in the nineteenth century.

"Hey, Hazel, this is funny—this farmer sold his oxen and it says here that they came back two weeks later, so he's put an ad in the paper asking the guy who bought 'em to come and get them."

"What?" Hazel had moved on from maps and was now leaf-ing through a book on local history published by the wife of a local clergyman in the early twentieth century.

"And remember what I was saying about how people in the old days made a lot of their own medicines? There's an ad here for Ballantyne's Sarsaparilla. They claim it will purify your blood and cure boils and tumours and ulcers and scurvy!"

Hazel shuddered. "Isn't there anything other than ads in those newspapers?"

"Sure. There's an article here about how to break oxen. Sounds cool but it turns out they mean *training* oxen to work in fields, like horses. And there's something about counterfeit money. Someone's been counterfeiting the twenty-five-cent note."

"Whoa. Big-time crook," Hazel said.

"Well, twenty-five cents was worth more back then." Ned set down the paper. "Hey, wouldn't it be cool to go back in time with a wad of cash from now, and buy up half the town?"

"I guess."

"I wouldn't want to have lived back then, though." Ned frowned. "I like all the stuff we have now: indoor plumbing, computers, medicine. There's a story here about this guy who had to have his leg amputated after it got infected."

There was silence for a while, as Hazel and Ned continued to read. The morning sun through the skylight and windows grew stronger, warming the library until the air felt thick and soporific. Hazel lay on her stomach, propped on her elbows, lost in the world of family feuds, recipes and gossip compiled by the clergyman's wife. The woman had a fondness for lurid tales of loss and woe—her local history seemed to focus on bankruptcies, swindlers and scams, deaths by drowning, runaway carriages and accidents of all sorts. There was even a story about an Irish American in a New York prison in 1920 confessing to a murder on Île du Loup nearly fifty years earlier. According to the clergyman's wife, the man, Connor Whelan, claimed to have killed a man for betraying the Fenian Brotherhood. Whelan had hidden the body and kept his crime a secret until making a deathbed confession out of remorse. Yet, according to the clergyman's wife, no one was sure just who he'd killed—or if he'd killed anyone at all. No body had ever been found on the island.

Somewhere a fly, woken by the sunshine, buzzed against a windowpane. Hazel rested her head on the history book, and wondered why anyone would confess to a crime they hadn't committed.

"Holy cow!" Ned jumped up as though he'd been stung. "Hazel, you've gotta see this."

Hazel scrambled to her feet. Ned pointed to a column of type halfway down the third page of the *Frontenac Gazette*. Hazel read, silently:

The Rose & River Inn has opened again for business. Authorities closed the establishment, on the banks of the Rose River, amid speculation it had become a gathering place for the Fenian Brotherhood. However, the charges could not be proven and the proprietor insists his family have always been Loyalists. He vows the inn will once again become a popular gathering place in Ville St-Pierre.

"The Rose & River Inn! That's got to be what the clue is talking about. Do you think maybe it still exists? Its flue has to be pretty old," Ned said.

"Maybe." Hazel's mind was whirling. "The Rose & River Inn . . . we've heard that name before."

"I don't think so. I'd remember."

Hazel snatched up the painter's diary. Was he the one who'd mentioned the inn?

"There!" She pointed in triumph. "See? Diary Guy was supposed to meet some Fenians there, to hand over that gift from his family."

"Huh. So maybe it really was a Fenian hangout. Let's check the other papers. Maybe we'll find something more about the

Rose & River Inn—like an address."

But although they pored over the tiny print for more than an hour, they found only one other reference to the inn, from a paper dated three months earlier than the copy Ned had read. A new well had been dug for patrons of the Rose & River Inn. The *Gazette* reported the quality of the drinking water at the inn had improved, owing to the new well having been dug farther away from the hog pen of a neighbouring farm.

But there was no address given for the inn and, as Hazel pointed out, even the farm was probably long gone.

It might have been the mention of hogs, but Hazel suddenly realized they'd worked straight through lunch. They replaced the maps and returned all their "evidence" to Hazel's room before making for the kitchen.

There was still no sign of Mark but Oliver and Deirdre were already home from school. The detritus of after-school snacks lay all around them—an open peanut butter jar, two milk glasses, nearly emptied, and the remains of a large bunch of grapes.

"Did you leave any food for us?" Ned asked.

"More important, we left room for dinner." Deirdre smiled. "Mark's gone into the village with Matt to pick up some ingredients. He's making steak and frites and he promised something special for dessert."

"The food at Land's End is definitely better than any restaurant," Ned said. "Hey, speaking of restaurants, have either of you ever heard of the Rose & River Inn?"

Deirdre nodded. "Sure. That's the place out by the retirement home. The place where they found the body."

CHAPTER SEVENTEEN

Hazel stared at Ned. He looked as stunned as she felt.

"No, wait—it wasn't a body, exactly," Deirdre was saying. "It was a skeleton. I think it was buried on the property. Hang on, there's a newspaper article around here somewhere, if it hasn't been recycled yet . . . Here it is. See for yourselves."

Historic Inn to Be Demolished

The recent finding of human remains at the Rose & River Inn will not postpone demolition of the historic building, authorities say.

Police were called in to investigate after a skeleton was found in the ruins of an old well on the property. However, the bones have now been turned over to archaeologists at Frontenac University, after a pathologist ruled they were over a hundred years old.

It was the latest in a series of delays that has plagued local developers seeking to build a condominium project on the land. Opponents of the development have long argued the inn should be preserved and turned into a museum. A small but vocal lobby group also sought the reopening of the inn's pub, The Boathouse. However, both buildings have decayed dramatically in the past few years and town council recently ruled it would cost too much to purchase and restore them. A spokesman for the consortium of developers said demolition would take place October 31.

"But that's tomorrow," Hazel said slowly. Their father couldn't possibly expect them to get the clue out by then. They were grounded, for pity's sake. Although, technically, one *could* argue they were grounded only until midnight tonight.

Mark's dinner was delicious, but Hazel could only pick at her meal. They were running out of time. The inn was going to be destroyed in just a few hours. What were they supposed to do? A condemned building—too decayed for the town council to save—sounded awfully dangerous. Surely their father and Charlotte wouldn't want them to go poking around in a place like that? It wasn't just dangerous, it was trespassing. They'd never ask Hazel and Ned to break the law . . . but the last couple of clues had seemed different. Hazel glanced across the table at Mark and realized he had just asked her a question.

"You kids haven't forgotten that Halloween is tomorrow?"

"Uh . . . nope?" Hazel tried to look interested.

"The party sounds hokey but it's actually a lot of fun," Deirdre said. "Everyone dresses up. They raise money for the village and even older kids go, so it's not like regular trick-or-treating where you're too old to go out if you're my age."

"I think you're too old to go out at *my* age," Oliver muttered. But Deirdre just patted his head.

"Oliver finds it all a bit too spooky," she said. "But we'll stick together and it'll be tons of fun. You'll see."

The rest of the evening was devoted to trying on all the

old costumes and dress-up clothes generations of Frumps had stashed away over the years. It was amusing, but by the time Hazel climbed the stairs to her bedroom that night, her mind was spinning.

What were she and Ned supposed to do now? The clue must be somewhere in the chimney flue of the old, abandoned Rose & River Inn, which they knew now was just outside the village, on Lunn Lane. Were Hazel and Ned really going to sneak inside the condemned building and find the last clue?

"Nothing about this makes sense." Hazel perched uneasily on the edge of her window seat. Beyond her window, the first stars shimmered faintly in the dark sky. She wondered how early a wrecking crew would arrive at the Rose & River Inn. If she and Ned wanted to get there first, they'd probably have to leave before dawn, just to be sure.

She was still sitting on the window seat when Ned knocked at the door.

"So, like they say in the movies," Ned began, "I have a very bad feeling about this."

Hazel nodded. "Me too. I've been sitting here trying to figure out whether we should go through with it."

"You think it's a trap?" Ned lowered his voice. "But why would Dad do that?"

"Unless it's not Dad." Hazel began to pace around the room. "It's funny. This whole treasure hunt started out pretty innocently. And then, with the last couple of clues, it's as if everything's changed. Like the sun was shining but all of a sudden it's grey and storm clouds are gathering."

"You're going to say we shouldn't go look for the flue clue," Ned said. "But that's not really *you* talking. That's some responsible, big-sister person." He punched her lightly on the shoulder. "I say we set our alarms and get up really, really early. We can borrow Oliver's and Deirdre's bikes, and get back before they have to leave for school."

"I don't know . . . I want to find out who's behind this just as much as you do, but what if something goes wrong? Uncle Seamus told us to stop!"

"If it looks dangerous, we'll just turn the bikes around and pedal to safety!" Ned said. "C'mon, Hazel. We can't quit now."

Hazel nodded slowly. "Okay, we'll go. But this time I want backup."

"We'll bring our cell phones. They may not work here at the castle but they seem to work everywhere else on the island."

"I'm thinking we need more than just phones." Hazel slapped a pad of paper down onto her desk and picked up a pen. "I say we leave a paper trail, just in case. I'll write a note explaining exactly where we've gone and why. You give it to Oliver. Tell him if we're not back by breakfast, he'd better open it and show it to everyone."

Ned nodded solemnly. "I'll have to tell him we have a mission before first light. He's a good soldier; he won't ask for details."

Hazel rolled her eyes.

She didn't feel quite so lighthearted the next morning when, just before dawn, she and Ned fastened their bike helmets and cast one last look at the castle where their cousins slept peacefully. Hazel still hadn't found her jacket, but she borrowed one of Deirdre's. And in their backpacks, she and Ned carried flashlights, cell phones, a length of rope, a bottle of water and a bag of cookies. They were as ready as they'd ever be.

They crossed Rose River in no time and made only one wrong turn before locating Lunn Lane.

It was going to be a lovely day. The earliest risers among the birds were already singing as the dawn sent its first pale streaks of pink across the sky. Gravel crunched underneath their tires. If she wasn't so nervous about getting in and out of the inn before it tumbled down around them, Hazel thought, she'd be enjoying the bike ride.

"I see it!" Ned pointed ahead to where the road curved, following the path of the river.

The Rose & River Inn looked far worse than its picture in the paper: it was a ruined island in a sea of waist-high weeds and fallen willow trees. The crumbling limestone building was so overgrown with vines, Hazel wondered if the ivy itself had pulled down some of the walls.

"This place looks more trashed than the lighthouse cottage," Ned said as he skidded to a stop beside a large wooden sign that warned: DANGER! KEEP OUT.

Hazel took off her helmet and looped its strap over the handlebars of Deirdre's bike. She glanced at her watch. "We'd better not waste any time."

They left their bikes leaning against an old sawhorse and waded into the weeds. The Rose & River Inn must have been a pretty sight a hundred years ago. In her mind, Hazel could picture all three storeys stripped of ivy and the gingerbread trim across the porch freshly painted.

"What's that over there?" Ned's voice broke through her reverie. "A barn?"

Hazel looked in the direction Ned was pointing. The remains of another stone-and-wood building were partly hidden behind a towering stand of pine trees.

"Could be a barn. Maybe a stable. But that reminds me—be careful where you step," she cautioned. "We don't know exactly where that old well is, the one where they found the bones. I wouldn't want you to fall in."

"Me neither. Anyway, we need to look out for two wells, right? Didn't the newspaper you found at the lighthouse say they dug a second well here, because the inn's patrons complained about the water? Yikes!"

"What?"

"Hazel, maybe the water went bad because of the skeleton! If somebody drowned in that first well, it would sure spoil the water."

"Okay, Ned, I have one word to say: *yuck*." Hazel tried to banish the image of a body decaying at the bottom of the well. It wasn't easy.

"Ow!"

"What now?"

"I just walked into an old berry patch with a zillion thorns. Go wide."

Hazel skirted the brambles while Ned with some difficulty disengaged himself. Zigging and zagging through the field, they arrived at the porch, their hands covered in scratches, their clothing covered in burrs.

"Nice." Ned picked several clumps of burrs out of his hair. "When this is all over, I'm going to have a serious talk with Dad. Or whoever sent us here. Hey, Hazel, where's all the equipment?"

"What equipment?" Hazel was tugging at the door. It couldn't be locked—what would be the point? But when she stepped back she could see the door frame was off kilter. They'd have to crawl in through a window.

"The newspaper said this place was going to be torn down today. Shouldn't there be trucks and a wrecking ball?"

"Yeah, I guess." Hazel had given up on the door and begun jimmying the window. Suddenly the sash gave way and the window slid up with a rattle. She had one leg through and was holding on to the window frame, about to swing the other leg over the sill, when she paused to consider Ned's words.

"You're right, this is strange." Hazel gazed across the empty field. "Maybe the newspaper got the date of the demolition wrong?"

She climbed the rest of the way into the room and stood for a moment, letting her eyes adjust to the dimness.

"Which means, maybe we didn't have to get up so early after all," Ned said as he clambered through the window after her.

Hazel could see now that the room in which they stood must have been a lobby. The furniture was long gone, but a carved wooden counter had been built into one of the walls.

"Or maybe we've been slower to solve the clues than Dad expected."

"I think we've solved the clues pretty quickly." Ned's voice came from somewhere behind her in the gloom.

It was a shame they weren't preserving any of the building. Despite the dust, the carved panels on the walls still looked elegant. On the other hand, the ceiling had fallen down in chunks, leaving heaps of plaster all over the floor, making Hazel think of a giant platter of meringue.

An enormous fieldstone fireplace stood at the back of the room. But as Hazel moved toward it, the floorboards beneath her feet creaked and shuddered.

"This place doesn't need a wrecking crew—it's falling apart all on its own," Ned observed. "Let's find the flue, grab the clue and get the heck out of Dodge."

"Working on it." Hazel took another step, but the sound of splintering wood filled the room. She hopped sideways, onto more solid flooring.

Ned stepped forward. "Maybe I should go first."

"I'm bigger and I weigh more than you—but I'm also the oldest. So I go first." Hazel took a deep breath and gingerly raised one foot and lowered it. So far so good. She took another step. Also good. Then another.

Crack. For a fraction of a second, Hazel thought, rifle shot. But it was the sound of a floorboard breaking in two. Hazel jumped back, dragging her foot and wincing as it scraped the rotten wood.

"That does it—I'm going in."

"Ned, wait!"

The panic in her voice stopped Ned halfway to the chimney. Around them the building creaked and groaned; shards of plaster tinkled down from above their heads and clouds of dust settled back onto the rotting floorboards.

Hazel took a deep breath. "Ned, *think*. If we can't make it safely across the room, neither could Charlotte or anyone else. And look around: there's no way anyone's been in this place for years. Everything's covered in dust."

Ned was silent for a moment. When he spoke, Hazel wasn't surprised to hear him argue.

"Someone *has* been in here. They must have come in a back way. I can see footprints near the fireplace."

Hazel could feel impatience bubbling up inside her. "Fine, someone has been here. But we can't get to the fireplace from this side of the room. It's just too dangerous. We'll have to go back out the way we came, and look for a side door."

Ned cleared his throat. "Actually," he said, "I don't think we should come back in here."

This time Hazel heard the tremor in her brother's voice. Dread formed in the pit of her stomach as she realized Ned hadn't moved in the past few minutes.

"Why not, Ned?"

"Look over there, and there, where the footprints stop."

Hazel peered into the dim recesses of the room. She thought she could see a small box beside the staircase, and another at the base of the chimney . . . and maybe another over there . . .

"Okay, I see them. What exactly am I looking at, Ned?"

"Explosives."

CHAPTER EIGHTEEN

"Are you sure? Are you sure those are explosives?"

From fifteen feet away, Hazel could hear Ned grind his teeth.

"Hey, I don't see Wile E. Coyote standing over there. But, yes, I *think* they're explosives. I really, *really* think. Do you seriously want to wait around and find out?"

Hazel took a deep, steadying breath before replying.

"No. Let's get out of here. Slowly, and quietly."

"No kidding."

Hazel stood her ground as Ned painstakingly retraced his steps. If the floorboards gave way and Ned fell into the cellar . . . But Hazel pushed the thought away. She'd just rescue him, that's all. She was getting pretty good at that.

Rescue him, or die trying?

But it didn't come to that. Ned made it to the window safely, and the instant his foot disappeared through the opening, Hazel bolted. Outside, she grabbed her brother's hand and ran and ran. They didn't stop until they reached the riverbank, gasping for breath.

The sunlight was painfully bright after the gloom of the inn. That had to be why Hazel's eyes watered. She gulped the fresh air and tried not to think about their narrow escape.

"It's irresponsible."

"What is?" Hazel looked at Ned. He was several shades paler than normal.

"The demolition guys. They can't leave explosives just lying around like that. There should be warning signs and a guard posted to keep people out."

"Yeah. But at least we're okay. I mean, we may not have the clue but we didn't blow up the building."

"You're setting a pretty high standard there, Hazel. At least we didn't detonate anything?" Ned replaced his spectacles and glared at the building. "It doesn't make sense: it *has* to be the inn."

Hazel suddenly realized that from the riverbank she could see the ruins of the barn from a different angle. A narrow column of stone towered over one end of the rubble.

"Uh, Ned, remember how we went to the wrong lighthouse?"

"You mean the *last* time I nearly died? Yeah, I remember."

"I think we just went to the wrong inn. At least, the wrong *part* of the inn. The newspaper said there was a pub, remember? The Boathouse. What if that ruined building over there isn't a barn—what if it was the pub?"

Ned groaned. "The clue said to look where the boat goes. Man oh man. That's sick."

"That's one word for it." Hazel put her arm around Ned's shoulders and squeezed gently. "Anyway, it makes more sense than Dad risking our lives at the inn. Come on."

The shortest way to the ruins was through a hawthorn thicket and a patch of nettles. By the time they reached the pine trees, Ned looked as if he'd lost a fight with an alley cat. Hazel could only assume she looked just as bad.

"Like the scrapes from that lighthouse weren't bad enough." Ned surveyed his hands. "Oh well—at least I'm consistent."

They surveyed the heap of stone and wood. Hard to believe it had once been a pub. At least there was no risk of explosives here; the building had collapsed in on itself and now was nothing more than a pile of rubble with the occasional remnant of wall. The chimney was the only part of the structure still intact. Still, they approached it with caution. When they were close enough to touch the chimney, Hazel grabbed Ned's arm and pointed. Wedged in a gap between the chimney's stones, barely within her reach, was the corner of an envelope.

Ned studied it pensively. "I just had this crazy thought. What if you pull it out and the whole chimney comes falling down on our heads?"

"This isn't a cartoon."

"Uh-uh. But just to be safe, maybe I should go wait over there."

Yet Ned stayed at her side as Hazel gently pried the paper from its hiding place. She started to rip open the envelope, but stopped and handed it to him. "Here. You saw the dynamite and got us out of there—you open it."

"Plastic explosives. Not dynamite," Ned said. "But okay."

With a flourish, he tore open the envelope and read:

To find the treasure I've hidden for you,
Just follow this final, simple clue:

There once was a castle library,
With a ring as red as a cherry.
It's behind a door,
Down near the floor,
Across from a portrait that's scary.
To the party you simply must go,

If my identity you want to know.
Bring me the jewel,
Lest I become cruel,
(I'll be the one dressed as a crow).

Sincerely, The Japer

"What's a japer?" Ned asked.

Hazel shrugged. "We can look it up when we get home." She scanned the clue again. "So the ring *is* part of this mystery."

"I know poetry's not my game, but doesn't this one seem pretty weak?"

Hazel nodded. "I don't think Dad wrote this. Or Charlotte."

Ned glanced at his watch. It was 7 a.m. "Yikes! We'd better pedal like our lives depend on it, Hazel, or we won't get home before Deirdre and Oliver read our note and sound the alarm."

They didn't talk much during the ride back to the castle. For one thing, they were aiming for speed. For another, they needed to ride in single file now that the island was awake and they were sharing the road with cars and tractors. Once in a while they'd holler at each other, straining their voices to be heard above the sounds of the wind on the lake, or the traffic.

"Maybe Dad just ran out of energy, so he couldn't be bothered to make it tricky or interesting anymore." Ned was riding in front. He turned his head slightly so he could be heard over the sound of gravel spitting up from their tires.

Hazel refrained from answering until they reached the bottom of the long slope that led up to the castle and could ride side by side. "Why does he say he might have to get cruel?"

"Yeah, that was disturbing." Ned crested the hill moments ahead of Hazel and leaped off Oliver's bike, letting it crash to the ground. "So maybe you're right and it isn't Dad writing the clues anymore. But if it isn't him, then who?"

Before Hazel could answer, the kitchen door burst open and Oliver, still in his pyjamas and robe, raced across the porch and down the steps toward them.

"We just finished reading your letter! Deirdre was about to call the cops!"

Hazel dropped Deirdre's bike and raced to the porch, hoping Deirdre hadn't started dialling yet. But the sandy-haired teenager met her on the veranda and wrapped her arms around Hazel so tightly she almost crushed the air out of her lungs.

"You're okay! We were so worried. I was just about to call the police or Dad . . ." Deirdre finally let go, and Hazel cautiously checked her ribs.

"But you didn't call the cops, did you?" Ned asked.

Deirdre shook her head.

"Is Matt upset?" Hazel glanced around, wondering why the twins weren't outside too.

"He doesn't know." Deirdre's face lost some of its glow. "The hospital called late last night—something about Charlotte. He hasn't come home yet. Mark woke me up half an hour ago and said he was going over there to find out what's happening."

Deirdre shivered. She was in her pyjamas too, but unlike Oliver, she hadn't put on a robe or slippers. "Can we go inside before I turn into an icicle?"

Once inside, Hazel expected Deirdre would start peppering them with questions and lecturing them about responsibility. She didn't anticipate that Deirdre would calmly put the kettle on for tea, set a platter of muffins on the table and then pick up the phone.

"No cops—don't worry. I'm just calling our schools."

Deirdre left messages explaining smoothly that, due to a

family emergency, the Frumps would not attend school that day. Then she sat and looked inquiringly at Hazel.

"I've been thinking for a long time that something was up with you two—something more than just this treasure hunt your Dad and Charlotte cooked up! So I want the complete 411. NOW. Don't leave anything out."

"Did you guys read the letter I gave Oliver?" Ned asked.

Deirdre made a face. "It has more holes than Oliver's socks. We want the whole story and we want it now. So spill. *Everything.*"

Telling everything took some time. Hazel hesitated when it came to revealing what they'd found in the library, but before she could stop him, Ned had produced the spell book, diary and the box of jewels. And soon, all the secrets were out.

Or almost all. Hazel was grateful that Ned didn't mention her dreams. The story was fantastical enough without any talk of hawks or illustrations coming to life.

"Well!" Deirdre reluctantly tore her eyes away from the ring. "I can't believe you guys managed to keep all this to yourselves."

"It wasn't easy," Hazel admitted. "But we thought Charlotte and Dad would be disappointed if they knew we'd found the jewels too soon. We still don't know if these are the lost jewels you guys were talking about, or the birthstones Dad said we'd find."

"Well, I'm emerald, and the twins are diamond, and Oliver's— what are you?" Deirdre looked at her brother, who shrugged.

"How should I know?"

"Pearl!" Deirdre pointed to the strand in the box. "He's pearl. So all our birthstones are here. This could be what Uncle Colin meant you to find. But they sure seem old enough to be the lost jewels."

"What's a japer?" Without waiting for an answer, Oliver seized the giant dictionary, flipping through the fragile pages so recklessly that Hazel flinched.

"Oh, here it is—a jape is a trick, a jest, a game. So I guess a japer is someone who does japes—like organizing a treasure hunt. Yeah, it says here: 'a trickster.'"

"Do the last few clues seem different to you?" Hazel asked hesitantly. "We wondered whether Dad and Charlotte got someone else to help . . . like maybe the twins?"

"I'm guessing Uncle Colin wrote most of them, but then Charlotte took over." Deirdre skimmed through the pile of clues again. "Yeah, my money's on Charlotte. Not Mark and *definitely* not Matt."

Deirdre glanced at the final clue again. "It's odd, though. You're supposed to bring the jewels to the Halloween party, where your dad will be dressed as a crow? That doesn't seem very likely, since he's in Europe."

"If Charlotte did take over writing the clues, she might be the one who was supposed to meet us at the party," Hazel said doubtfully. "But then, I'm not sure there's any point in going, now that she's in hospital."

"We could ask her, except Matt says she doesn't remember anything that happened after Thanksgiving." Deirdre looked at the phone. "I hope they call soon."

No one spoke for a few moments. Then Oliver shivered.

"It's kind of creepy to think about some of this stuff lying around in our library for more than a century."

"I wish we knew where the spell book and the journal come in," said Hazel. "I thought maybe the last clue would explain, but it doesn't mention them."

"Maybe your dad and Charlotte don't know about them." Deirdre fingered the journal gently. "Maybe you were right to think they weren't part of the treasure hunt."

The room fell silent again. No one wanted to say it, but Hazel could tell from the way they all kept glancing at the phone that everyone shared her growing anxiety over the lack of word from Matt and Mark. What could be happening? Wasn't Charlotte supposed to be on the mend?

Deirdre set her tea mug down with an overly loud *thud*.

"Let's go to the library—you guys can show us exactly where you found this stuff."

As diversions go, it wasn't bad. In the library, Hazel demonstrated how the secret compartments in the baseboards worked, and understood why both her cousins insisted on getting down on their bellies to peer into the openings, making sure she and Ned hadn't missed anything. Hazel watched from below as first Deirdre and then Oliver scaled the second-storey ladder, inspected the compartment and confirmed, regretfully, that nothing else was hidden behind the plaque.

"Who on earth would have hidden that journal?" Deirdre said as she descended the circular stairs. She flopped down onto one of the leather armchairs and stared up at the words. "And why hide it all the way up there?"

"It's the only other secret compartment in the room—trust me, we looked everywhere," Ned said.

"I think whoever put it there was trying to send a message by hiding it behind the word *silence*," Hazel said.

Oliver contemplated the portrait. "I wonder why they don't match. I mean, which one got changed—the plaque or the portrait?"

Deirdre was leafing through the journal, a frown creasing her brow. "You know how you said the last couple of entries were just gibberish?"

Hazel and Ned nodded.

"I don't think they are. I think they're in code."

"Code?" Oliver peered over Deirdre's shoulder. "How can you tell?"

"Well, not code exactly. A code is when you use words or

phrases to represent other words or phrases. This looks more like a cipher. Probably a basic substitution cipher—like a Caesar cipher."

Deirdre liked word puzzles. In the summer, Deirdre had been the first one to realize that Clive Pritchard was using anagrams to create aliases.

"So what exactly is a cipher?" asked Oliver.

"It's a way of encrypting messages, but it gives you a lot more flexibility than a code."

Hazel tried to look as if she understood. Deirdre laughed.

"Okay, think of it this way—for a code, you need a code *book* or you're sunk."

"Why?"

"Because a code is random. That's the whole point. You need a code book to tell you that 'Elvis is in the building' really means: 'Look out—the principal's coming.' But a cipher is like a key to unlock the encrypted message. You don't need a book to translate the message—you just need to know what formula to use. Like, certain numbers represent certain letters. Or, maybe certain letters represent other letters."

Hazel was hopelessly lost. She looked at Ned and Oliver to see if they were still following. To her irritation both boys were clearly way ahead of her.

"So you could use the number five to represent the letter *E*, and maybe number three to represent the letter *P*," Ned said. "That way, *HELP* becomes H5L3."

"Or you could use symbols for some letters," Oliver suggested. "So instead of *HELP* you write #E%P."

"Sure." Deirdre fished around in Hazel's backpack and pulled out a notebook and a pencil. "Now, this journal looks like a classic Caesar cipher. It shifts all the letters in the alphabet by three. So *A* becomes *D* and *B* becomes *E*."

Deirdre scribbled as she spoke. She turned the pad around

so Hazel could see. "With a Caesar cipher, *HELP* becomes KHOS."

"What do you do when you get to the end of the alphabet?" Hazel asked. "What's *Z*?"

Ned and Oliver looked at her with pity in their eyes. But Deirdre just nodded.

"That's a fair question. The last three letters of the alphabet roll over to the beginning. So, *X* becomes *A* and *Y* becomes *B* and *Z* would be *C*."

"Oh." It sounded like a lot of work to Hazel. She couldn't imagine using a cipher to write anything longer than a sentence. Wouldn't most people get bored and give up after a few words?

"We could decipher this pretty easily." Deirdre was chewing on the end of her pencil as she stared at the journal. "I really think it's a straight Caesar cipher—no modifications." She glanced up at Hazel. "You know, like if you really wanted to get fancy you'd switch it up here and there—follow the cipher most of the time, but do something different for the fifth letter in every word, or the third word in every sentence."

Hazel's head hurt. She hoped Deirdre wasn't going to suggest she help translate the journal.

"Why don't we each take a paragraph?" Deirdre said. "It would go faster. But we can't all work from the book at the same time. I'll copy out a paragraph for each of you on a separate piece of paper."

Hazel nodded glumly. She figured she wanted to know what was in the diary as much as the next guy. Except, the next guys were Ned and Oliver and they'd be much faster at this kind of thing.

When Deirdre handed the sheets around, Hazel saw to

her relief that she had the shortest paragraph. But she'd still have to concentrate if she didn't want to keep everyone else waiting.

For the next few minutes the only sound in the library was that of four pencils scratching across paper.

Deirdre was the last to lay down her pencil, but Hazel sneaked a peak and saw that she'd given herself the longest section. Then Deirdre collected the papers, as if they'd just finished a pop quiz, and shuffled them into order.

"Okay, here goes." She cleared her throat and began to read:

I am a prisoner at Land's End. I fear for my life. Edwin Cornelius Frump has revealed his true self: he is mad. He believes himself to be a witch. He carries about his person a book in which he composes spells and magical rites. It is utter nonsense, but he believes that he has special power and he trusts his incantations.

He is surely no witch but he is indeed the thief. He took my belongings to use them in the practice of his witchcraft. It would be amusing if my situation was not so dire.

His sister, Mercy, did settle their debt, with some valuable jewels. I returned to my rooms to collect my things and leave this accursed place, as agreed. Yet before I could depart, a servant arrived with a note that claimed to be from Mercy. Alas! When I responded by descending to the parlour as invited, I found only Edwin in the room. He told me his sister would soon be joining us and offered me tea and cakes. Thinking to humour him, I partook of his hospitality. Before long the room began to swim before my eyes. I felt my consciousness slipping away, but I had time to leave a clue for Mercy. She alone knows of the mission my family entrusted to me. She knows I would not leave this accursed place without the gift for the Fenians. I slipped the precious jewel from

*my pocket and slid it beneath the cushion of my chair. I pray
she will find it and come to help me.*

*I do not know what happened next. I only know that when
I awoke I found myself locked in a room with no windows.*

Hazel gasped. She could tell Ned was thinking the same
thing: the painter had been imprisoned in the room she'd
stumbled upon when they were searching for the second clue!
But Deirdre was still reading.

*It is a hideous place—Edwin has been using it as a sort of
storage room for the bodies of the animals he uses in his taxidermy. The smells are wretched. I have only one lamp and I
light it sparingly, as my supply of oil is running out.*

Deirdre paused. "Guess you're glad none of that stuff was
still there when you fell through the trap door!"
Hazel grimaced, and Oliver sent her a sympathetic glance.
But there was more. Deirdre continued:

*Luckily I carry my journal with me, and Edwin himself left
a pen behind in this forsaken place. I write this note using a
cipher in hopes that, should a terrible fate befall me, perhaps
my words will survive. I do not know what Edwin has in
store for me. I can only hope that his sister Mercy will learn
of his misdeeds and come to my rescue. I fear she will think
I simply departed, as we agreed. My hopes are pinned on
the jewel. If Mercy finds it, she will know I did not leave.
In the meantime I shall try to reason with Edwin when he
reappears. Perhaps he will prove a Fenian sympathizer and
might be persuaded to let me go, that I might carry out my*

mission. That is, if he ever returns. I pray that he does. I do
not wish to die here alone.

A chill had fallen over the room. No one spoke. Hazel could see her own horror reflected in the others' faces. So she wasn't the only one to jump when the library door creaked open.

CHAPTER NINETEEN

"Whoa!" Deirdre leaped out of her chair and stood staring at her older brothers. Hazel let out her breath slowly. She'd half-expected Edwin Frump to walk into the room; it was a relief to see Mark in his Lucky Dube T-shirt and jeans, and Matt in his neatly pressed khakis.

"Why so jumpy?" Mark strode over to the table and ruffled Oliver's hair. "You kids look like you've seen a ghost."

Oliver threw his arms around Mark and hugged him, almost knocking his older brother to the ground. Ned looked as if he wanted to do the same.

"No ghost," Hazel said. "But we *are* a bit creeped out. You just yanked us back into the twenty-first century."

"Hold that thought. As intriguing as that sentence is, we need to talk about something else first." Matt looked at Deirdre. "Why aren't you and Oliver in school?"

Deirdre exploded. "Why aren't we in school? What's the matter with you guys? Why didn't you phone? We've been worried sick about Charlotte! You said you'd call!"

"I did call," said Matt. "I called the school and asked to speak with you. They seemed a little surprised that I didn't know about the family emergency that was keeping you and Oliver home."

"Oh." Deirdre deflated as quickly as if she'd been stuck with a pin. "Well, okay. So how is Charlotte, anyway?"

"She's fine." Mark gently disengaged himself from Oliver's grip. "Truly—it looked bad last night, there was some kind of infection, but it's all okay now. So . . . does someone want to tell us what's been going on here?"

"Okay." Deirdre gave an exaggerated sigh. Glancing at Hazel and Ned for approval, she began spreading out all the clues and books on one of the library tables. "It's going to take a while. And it'll be easier if we can show you some things as we go."

"Excellent." Mark rubbed his palms together. "They just don't have enough show-and-tell at university."

Hazel didn't really want to go through everything again, so she let Deirdre tell the story, with Ned jumping in occasionally when Deirdre left something out or got a detail wrong.

"I'm not surprised the treasure hunt got you into trouble." Matt sifted through the pile of clues, examining first one, then another.

Mark nodded. "Oliver, you would have been too little to remember, but when we were kids and Charlotte would babysit, she loved to make up clues and riddles. Once I remember she wrote a clue that had to do with McCormack's window display. Remember how grumpy that guy got at us, Matt? Just for standing outside on the sidewalk, looking in."

"That wasn't the only time one of Charlotte's treasure hunts got us into trouble."

"Yeah . . . but most of them were fun." Mark smiled at the memory.

Matt held the ring up to catch the light. "I don't know much about jewels, but this is one whopping big stone. If it's a real ruby it's got to be worth a fortune."

"It could be a garnet," Deirdre said. "I read somewhere that they were popular in Victorian times."

"What makes you think it's Victorian?" Mark asked.

"We sent photos of it to our neighbour Frankie and she showed it to a bunch of jewellery experts online," Ned said. "They thought it was probably real—and definitely antique."

"And there are those encrypted entries at the end of the creepy journal," Deirdre said. "Mercy Frump paid off the portrait painter with jewels. It's a pretty big coincidence."

"Speaking of coincidences, there's one more thing you all should know." Hazel took a deep breath. "Frankie got an e-mail from someone who wanted to buy the jewels. She said her name was Vera Thirdcclip. With two 'c's.'"

Hazel looked around the room, but no one registered anything beyond polite interest.

"Okay, well, Deirdre will probably work this out much faster than I did, but I might as well tell you now: that's an anagram for Clive Pritchard."

It was as if Hazel had lobbed one of Ned's stink bombs across the room. Her cousins' expressions ranged from horrified to sick. And the hubbub that ensued, as everyone talked over top of everyone else, seemed as if it would last forever. Finally, Hazel put her fingers in her mouth and let out a shrill whistle. That did the trick.

"Even if Vera really is Clive Pritchard, he may just have found out about the jewels through Sketchbook," Hazel said. "He knows lots of people in the art world; one of them could have sent Frankie's e-mail to him. But what I want to know is, what do we do now?" Hazel looked around the room.

Ned grabbed a blank sheet of paper and a pen. "It's like a Venn diagram."

Hazel groaned. "No. Don't start talking math. I don't remember exactly what a Venn diagram is."

Ned ignored her. He drew a circle. Then he drew another circle, overlapping the first. In the overlapping section Ned wrote the word: *jewels*.

"See, the circle on the right represents the treasure hunt," he explained. "And the circle on the left is the old books—the spell book and the journal. What's sort of confusing is the jewellery, because it seems to relate to both sets."

"Sets?" Hazel asked.

"The circles," Ned said. "Each circle represents a set. I'm just showing how they connect. The clues and the books have nothing to do with each other, as far as we know. Only the jewels are a part of each set."

"Or each circle?" Hazel said tentatively. She figured her head would explode if Ned said no. But he just smiled and nodded.

Mark had both the spell book and the journal open in front of him. "Okay, so we have two mysteries here. And for some reason, the jewels turn up in both. But the treasure hunt's a dead end—you solved all the clues, and the only thing left to do is hit that party and see what happens. So for now we might as well concentrate on the historical mystery."

"I think so too," said Matt. "It bothers me that the journal stops so abruptly."

Deirdre looked sober. "What do you think happened to the painter?"

"He escaped," Oliver said in a hopeful tone. "We've never found any mummified corpses in any of the towers, right?"

"Right. I'm sure Edwin Frump wasn't really evil." Deirdre adopted the same tone. "Maybe he was just playing a practical joke. A really bad practical joke."

Hazel shook her head. "You think he suddenly says, 'Just kidding,' and lets Diary Guy go?" She shivered, picturing their grinning ancestor sneaking into the painter's bedroom in the middle of the night. "Get real."

Matt nodded. "If the painter is telling the truth in his journal, Edwin Frump slipped him some kind of knockout drug and then kidnapped him. That's no joke."

"It bothers me too." Ned sounded distracted.

Hazel glanced across the table at her brother. "What bothers you?"

"The journal. It's like Matt said, it doesn't make any sense for it to stop there."

"Sure it does." Mark shrugged. "The painter guy could have escaped, like Oliver said, and he just left his book behind. Or I suppose crazy Edwin could have killed him."

"Hey!" Deirdre said. "You're scaring Oliver."

"No, he isn't," said Oliver, who had turned very pale.

"Fine, he's scaring *me*," Deirdre said. "Nobody killed anyone. You're talking about our ancestors. Don't be ridiculous."

"But if Edwin killed the painter, then who hid the painter's journal?" Matt asked.

"And why hide it at all?" Ned said. "Why not destroy it? It's evidence."

"Well, it's circumstantial evidence." Mark rubbed his chin. "It doesn't *prove* Edwin Frump killed the portrait painter. It just looks bad."

"So why keep it around?" Ned asked.

"Could you all please stop talking about killing?" But doubt had crept into Deirdre's voice.

"It's not the only thing that looks bad." Hazel picked up the ring. "If Mercy gave the jewellery to the painter as a way to pay off the family's debt, how come it's still here? He wouldn't have left without it—he made a big deal in his journal about needing money."

"I'm guessing he didn't leave," Oliver said in a small voice.

Deirdre frowned. "It's horrible to think something like this could have happened here—even if it was a long time ago."

"But why keep the book?" Ned asked again. "Why keep it, if that's all there is?"

Matt gave him a quizzical look. "What do you mean?"

"It only makes sense to keep the journal, to preserve it, if someday you want people to see it," Ned said. "Whoever hid it didn't want the journal found back then, but they did want it to be found eventually. They wanted the truth to come out someday."

"*Veritas* versus *silentium*." Mark paused. "They wanted us to know that silence had replaced truth."

Ned nodded. "But the journal doesn't tell the whole story. We don't know how it ends. The person who hid it should have done something else— like write a letter to go with it. Otherwise, what's the point?"

Mark stretched and stood up. "Fair enough. So let's go check the secret compartment again and see what you guys missed."

"We didn't miss anything," Hazel said wearily. "Ask Deirdre and Oliver—they checked too, just before you got here."

But Mark and Matt wanted to see for themselves, so Deirdre and Oliver volunteered to show them the hidey-holes. Tired of show-and-tell, Hazel volunteered to head to the kitchen to start laying the table for lunch. Ned followed, pausing first to pluck the diary and the spell book from the table.

As Hazel organized drinking glasses, cutlery and plates, Ned sat leafing through the books. He moved from the spell book to the journal and then back again, lost in thought.

After a few minutes he glanced up at Hazel. "We're agreed it was Mercy's book before it was Edwin's, right? She was the one whose spells made sense."

"Right." Hazel rinsed a bunch of grapes and set them in a bowl beside him. Now what? Mark would handle the cooking, but she needed to do something with her hands. She began to wash a few of the breakfast dishes. "We decided the earlier spells were more like first aid or medicines made from herbs, and it makes sense that the bizarre stuff must have been added by Edwin after he got hold of the book."

"So what if she understood more than plants—what if Mercy had a better understanding of basic chemistry than her brother did?"

Hazel put down the dishtowel to stare at Ned. "What are you talking about?"

Ned acted as if he hadn't even heard her. He picked up the book and walked toward the stove.

"Whoa. What are you doing with that?"

Behind his spectacles, Ned blinked. "Don't worry, I'm not going to hurt the book. I just need to heat it up for a minute."

"Excuse me?"

Ned said nothing. He had turned one of the burners on low and was holding the journal above the stovetop, open to the blank page. Hazel gulped. This was dangerous.

"Hey, you know when grown-ups say, 'Kids, don't try this at home'?" Hazel said. "This is what they mean. Turn the stove off, Ned. NOW."

But Ned had already switched off the burner and was frowning at the book.

"Okay. Not heat-activated. Let's try . . . well, vinegar of course, that's an obvious one. But maybe . . . Hey, Hazel, could you boil some cabbage?"

"Sure." Hazel took her brother by the shoulders and steered him back to the table. She pushed him down into a chair. "Ned, stop freaking me out."

"Oh. Sorry. Invisible ink." Ned looked as if that was explanation enough. He tried to get up.

Gently but firmly Hazel held him down. "What *about* invisible ink?"

"Mercy was a scientist, Hazel, an amateur scientist. And she would have wanted the truth to come out eventually." Ned looked down at the book in his hands. "I'm guessing she found the journal and she figured out the cipher. And maybe that inspired her. She'd write a secret entry to finish the journal so that someday, someone would find it and then the whole story could be told."

"So you think Mercy wrote in the painter's journal," Hazel said, "in invisible ink?"

Ned nodded. "She was smart, Hazel. She was smart enough to teach herself about healing plants and smart enough to know Edwin was nuts. Why wouldn't she be able to make some kind of invisible ink? *Everyone* knows how to do that. It's not rocket science."

Hazel winced. "Um . . . I don't know how to make it."

"Oh." Ned looked as if he'd finally remembered who he was speaking to. "Well, there are a lot of different ways to make invisible ink. She could have used juice or milk or vinegar. But there's tons of other stuff."

"And you make the invisible ink visible again by heating up the paper?" Hazel didn't even bother asking Ned how he knew all this. If he could make near-lethal stink bombs and cause unending hiccups, he could handle invisibility.

"Obviously after the ink dries you need to do *something* to make it visible again. These days most of the common invisible inks react to ultraviolet light. But somebody making her own ink, more than a hundred years ago . . . I would have thought she'd go for a heat-activated solution."

"Well, of course. Who wouldn't?"

Ned ignored her. "But it didn't react to being held over the stove, so I'm guessing we have to look at pH indicators. Mercy would have used something acidic or basic. So we add a pH indicator and the indicator will turn colour when it touches the ink."

"Of course, pH indicators." Hazel rested her head on the table. "Could you just pretend I know what you're talking about, and skip the details? It'd be faster."

"Sure." Ned nodded matter-of-factly. "You'll learn about all this in high school, anyway. In the meantime, I think we should just start by assuming Mercy made her ink using something that wasn't too hard for her to get her hands on. Let's keep it simple."

"Oh yes. Let's."

Ned drummed his fingers on the table. Hazel waited.

"Corn starch," he decided. "Let's start with that. It would have been handy—just lying around the kitchen, not something she'd have to get from a chemist."

"Okay." Hazel crossed the room to the cupboard where Matt kept the baking supplies and began rummaging around, looking for a small cardboard box.

"Sorry." Ned shook his head. "I meant, let's assume Mercy used something like corn starch to make her ink. To make it visible again we'll need, uh, iodine."

Hazel sighed. "So, medicine cabinet, not kitchen cabinet?"

"Right."

By the time Hazel returned, all the cousins had joined Ned in the kitchen. From the eager expressions on their faces, Hazel could tell Ned had already briefed them on his plan. She handed the bottle to Ned and watched as he mixed drops of iodine with water in a glass jar. He dipped the corner of a cloth into the solution and gingerly daubed at the blank page. Like magic, shaky, dark blue letters—almost black—began to appear. There were spaces here and there, where letters, or entire words, were missing. But the cousins were able to make out most of what was written.

I, Mercy Frump, believe that my br ther, Edwin C nelius Frump, may have been r sponsible for the death of the young

*man who owned this bo k, Mr. Kenton P   , who was at
L nd's En to paint a series of portraits. Mr. P. has not be n
seen for a year.*

*I cannot prove that Edwin murd ed Mr. P. but I found
this diary many mont s after I was told he had lef our h me.
I am convinc d he would not have l ft it beh nd. I searched
our home for other clues but found n hing. Unt l yesterday,
in the east parl   r. Among the c shions, I found*

*It was the same ring Mr. P. showed to me more than a
year ago. It is very distinctive, with a large ruby that daz-
zlcs the beholder. He was to pass the ring to a member of
the Fenian Brotherhood. He never let it out of his sight. My
discovery fil ed me with dread and I h stened to conf ont my
b other. He took the ring and made it d sappear, I   not know
how. Edwin has latel taken to practi ing silly tri ks he calls
magic. Now he denies there ever wa   a ring.*

*My brother must be pr tected from hims lf and the world
must also be protected from Edwin. I will arrange for him to
be c mmitted to the care of an ins   ution in England. For
the sake of our reputation, I will let it be known that Edwin
has gone abroad to study taxidermy. Then I will do my best to
learn the fate of Mr. P. It is the least I can do for his family.*

"So, the ring you found belonged to Diary Guy. I mean, Kenton
P." Mark shook his head. "Poor guy—we may never know exactly
what happened to him, but it doesn't look good."

"Maybe there's another entry?" Deirdre looked at Ned.

But even though he daubed the iodine and water solution
on every remaining page, no more words appeared.

"She might have written another entry later on," Ned said.
"The next batch of ink she used might have been too weak to
last all this time."

"Well, what do we do now?" asked Oliver.

"I think we need to decide about the treasure hunt, and this Halloween party." Hazel looked around the room. "It's in a few hours. Do we go?"

"About that," Mark began, "I'm not the only one here who thinks it's crazy to bring valuable jewels to a giant, crowded costume party, right?"

"This whole thing still strikes me as crazy," Matt said. "That pioneer village is a zoo at Halloween. There are too many people and there's no security—remember two years ago when vandals trashed some of the buildings? When Dad asked us to keep an eye on things here, I don't think *this* is what he had in mind."

"Relax, bro. We'll stick together. I say we leave the jewels at home, but we go—just to see if any crows show up." Mark rubbed his hands together. "It'll be fun."

"What if Clive Pritchard *is* involved somehow? What if he shows up dressed as a crow?" Ned asked.

"He's in jail, and he's staying there," Matt said. "I'm not worried about running into Pritchard. But I would like to see if anyone else turns up to claim that ring."

Hazel heard the determination in Matt's voice and glanced across the table at her cousin. She liked Matt, but it was all too easy to dismiss him as the older brother, the neat freak, the responsible one. When his adventurous streak broke through, it tended to catch her unawares.

"Now probably isn't the best time to mention this," Hazel began reluctantly, "but after Ned got hurt at the lighthouse, Uncle Seamus told us to stop the treasure hunt."

"Wait, technically, he said the treasure hunt 'should be' cancelled," Ned said. "He never said it *was* cancelled."

There was a long silence. Everyone looked at Matt.

"Dad's a lawyer," Matt said finally. "He chooses his words with care. If he said the hunt *should be* cancelled, he was expressing an opinion . . . and that's not the same thing as giving an order."

Another long silence.

"You mean we can go?" Hazel could see the shock she felt mirrored on Ned's face.

"We can go. But we're leaving early, before it gets wild." Matt looked around the room as if daring anyone to challenge him.

"We never decided what to wear," Mark said. "Anybody got any suggestions about our costumes?"

Deirdre had a crazed look in her eye. "I know! Four of us could go as a bunch of meddling kids, and Ned could be Scooby-Doo. Oliver, you could be that other dog, what was his name?""

"Scrappy-Doo." Oliver shook his head. "That was a dark time in the cartoon world."

"Matt should be Velma," Mark said.

But in the end, they agreed the simplest thing would be to go as ghosts. There were plenty of old sheets in the castle, and the disguise was so corny they'd likely be the only people to use it.

"That'll make it easier to keep track of each other," Mark said. "Don't look so worried, Hazel. We'll get in, get candy, and get out. If we stick together, what could go wrong?"

CHAPTER TWENTY

When they arrived at the Halloween party, Hazel understood Oliver's hesitation. The first thing she saw was a row of what appeared to be severed heads mounted on the pickets of a high wooden fence that encircled the pioneer village.

"This place is seriously disturbed," she murmured. Ned agreed.

At boarding school, they celebrated Halloween with a masquerade ball and the teachers got up a haunted house that was so corny it couldn't scare even the youngest students. And back in the city, when Hazel and Ned were younger, they'd trick-or-treated among friends. They never encountered anything scary at their neighbours' apartments or downstairs at Monsieur Gentil's café.

But entering the gate at the pioneer village, Hazel felt as if she were stepping into a different world. It was so dark and windswept and alien. And overrun with adults and children in truly horrible disguises.

At the gate, they traded their tickets for fluorescent trick-or-treat pails and a handful of glow-sticks. Ned asked Oliver what the sticks were for, and Oliver explained they were safer than candles.

"Wouldn't flashlights be even better?" Ned asked, narrowly avoiding tripping over a tree root.

"You'd think," Matt agreed sardonically. "But people complained that they ruined the effect. Not spooky enough."

As they made their way along the footpath, they passed the open door of the blacksmith's forge; a blazing fire hissed and crackled inside. The blacksmith himself stood in the doorway. Attired in devil's horns and cape, he cast a terrifying shadow across the lawn. Beside him, his assistant bent over an anvil, sending a shower of sparks streaking into the night as he hammered a stick of red-hot steel. The light from the forge briefly illuminated a horde of passing goblins and ghouls drenched in fake blood, before they disappeared down the path, the darkness swallowing them whole.

"Oh yeah," Ned said. "I can see how this place might not seem spooky enough."

They all stayed together at first, keeping their eyes open for someone dressed as a crow, just as the clue had said. Mark and Matt had decided Charlotte must have roped a friend into helping. They'd rummaged around the castle until they found a trick box in which they placed a dime-store ring. The lid of the box snapped shut on your finger if you tried to take the ring out, and Mark was looking forward to handing it over to the crow.

The village, with its log cabins and board-and-batten shops, was meant to evoke the nineteenth century. But Hazel couldn't help thinking of an earlier era, a time when villagers might rise up in fear against a woman just because she knew some first aid, or lived alone, with a cat for companionship. A time of witch trials, hangings and burnings. Deirdre touched her shoulder gently, and Hazel nearly jumped out of her high-top basketball shoes.

"Sorry, just wanted to point out my gym teacher! That's her, dancing over by that bonfire. Some disguise, eh? She really *is* a witch."

Just then, Oliver spied a skinny crow, about Charlotte's height, near the tinsmith's shop. "It's the japer!"

He was dressed all in black, with black combat boots on his feet and his arms concealed beneath shiny black capelike folds of cloth that vaguely suggested wings. Hazel thought that they were definitely a more practical choice than giant feathered appendages. And with a mask like that, the crow could afford to keep the rest of his costume simple. Hazel couldn't take her eyes off his slick black feathers and dark, glassy eyes. Even his beak looked cruel. He was a crow, all right. A creepy, menacing nightmare of a crow.

"Let's get him!" Oliver cried.

But before anyone could move, Ned pointed to another crow heading toward the bakery. And then Deirdre grabbed Hazel's arm as a third crow went by on the hay wagon, sitting beside three blind mice.

Every scary movie Hazel had ever seen shared one single idea: *splitting up is bad*. And the Frumps had vowed to stick together. But there were simply too many crows. So Oliver and Matt followed the first crow, while Deirdre, who ran cross-country, and Mark (who always believed he was fitter than he actually was) took off after the wagon.

Hazel and Ned followed the bakery crow.

Keeping their crow in sight, but never quite catching up, they followed it past the bakery and down a narrow, twisting path that wound through the woods toward a tiny chapel painted a ghostly white. Once, Hazel thought the crow looked over its shoulder—to make sure they were following? They hung back, then, letting a few trick-or-treaters come between them and the crow.

"This is nuts. He's leading us all over the place," Hazel said. "Isn't 'as the crow flies' supposed to be the fastest way to get someplace?"

"This is a crow *walking*, remember? Anyway, don't start

with the crow jokes or we'll be here until you're covered in wrinkles . . . you know, crow's feet?"

Hazel groaned. "Hey, what do you call a bunch of crows, anyway? A flock? A herd? Don't they have some unusual name?"

"Beats me. Hey!" Ned tugged on Hazel's sheet. "Look at that. Am I seeing double?"

Their crow had suddenly stopped. It was standing stock-still and staring. Just a few feet away stood another crow—about the same height and build, and wearing the identical costume, the identical mask.

"We can't split up," Hazel whispered. "After all, both these crows can't be the japer. Let's just pick one and follow it."

"We *have* to split up." Ned's tone was scathing. "Like you said, both these crows can't be the japer. You pick one and follow it. I'll take the other."

"Ned, don't be silly. This place is crazy. It's like some deeply disturbed version of Mardi Gras. I can't let you wander around in the dark, all by yourself, following some strange grown-up in a freaky crow costume."

"You're not the boss of me! Besides, I can handle myself."

"Oh, fine then. Off you go."

Ned actually took a step forward, but Hazel grabbed a handful of ghost costume, along with hair, and yanked.

"Ow."

"I was being sarcastic." Hazel reached down and grabbed Ned's hand. "We're staying together: I don't care how many crows there are."

Ned grumbled, but he didn't try to pull away. Just then, seven dwarves swarmed past Hazel and Ned. Buffeted by waves of four-year-olds in beards, hollering, "Heigh-ho, Heigh-ho!" Hazel tried to stand her ground, but one of the dwarves trod on the corner of her ghost sheet, yanking her backward. Hazel stumbled, tripped over the plastic axe dragged by another dwarf, and fell, sprawling on the ground, taking two small, bearded people with her. The forest rang with cries of alarm. Hazel looked up into the cold, unforgiving eyes of Snow White, arms folded across her chest, foot tapping.

"Connor, Emma, don't cry. I'm sure this nice ghost will help you pick up your candy. Won't you, Ghost?"

"Sure." Hazel sighed. "C'mon, Ned—let's get this picked up."

But Ned was gone. And so were the crows.

Hazel had never cleaned up anything so fast in her whole life. Within moments, Connor, Emma and the rest of the troop were scampering off down the path, and she was alone.

Completely alone.

It was impossible to know which way Ned had gone. She'd just have to guess. But as Hazel started down the path again, the darkness seemed to close in on her. She reached into her trick-or-treat bag and groped for the glow-stick to light her way, but the bag was empty.

"Connor! You little thief," she muttered.

She could see the shoemaker's hut up ahead. From what Hazel remembered of the map that Mark had shown her earlier, that hut was at the farthest edge of the pioneer village near the maize maze.

The sounds of the trick-or-treaters receded into the distance; around her now Hazel could hear the trickle of water over stones and the wind sighing in the leaves. A twig snapped beneath her foot and the noise startled an animal in the underbrush—she could hear it scurrying away. Branches crowded Hazel's path. She was nearly at the hut now, but the door was closed and she could see no candles or lanterns. It was deserted. She turned to retrace her steps.

A hawk swooped in front of her, freezing Hazel in her tracks. He perched on a branch of the tree nearest her and gazed at her in silence.

"What?" Hazel whispered. "I need to find Ned."

The hawk soared into the air over Hazel's head, landing on the roof of the shoemaker's hut behind her. Taking it as a sign, Hazel crept to the door and listened. Someone was inside. She could hear voices: kids, not grown-ups.

"I don't know what to do. This is so messed up."

Hazel stiffened. She knew that frightened whine. It belonged to Kenny Pritchard. There was a loud sniff, followed by a muffled sound that suggested the wiping of his nose on his sleeve.

"The park's gonna close for winter soon—you could hide out here in this hut, and I could smuggle you food. We've always got leftovers."

"I can't live here. It's cold and there's no TV or PlayStation or anything. You're such a moron, Billy. I don't even know why I'm friends with you."

Yes, that was Kenny, all right. And his sidekick, Billy. Hazel glanced up at the hawk, still perched on the edge of the roof. She had things to do: she had to find Ned, her cousins, the japer. Why exactly was she here?

"*I'm* a moron? I'm not the one who told your uncle about the stupid treasure hunt! I'm not the one who switched the clues."

So it was Clive Pritchard again, only this time with Kenny following his orders instead of Kenny's dad. Hazel's hands balled into fists. Those Pritchards.

But much of her fury was directed inward. She should have known it was Clive. It made perfect sense. Thanks to Charlotte, Kenny knew about the treasure hunt. Thanks to Kenny, Clive Pritchard knew. Both Kenny and his uncle clearly had too much time on their hands, but tampering with the clues was just the sort of mischief the Pritchards could sink their teeth into. Hazel could easily imagine Clive getting Kenny to leave clues that would take them into more and more dangerous places.

He wouldn't worry about putting Kenny in danger. That might even be part of the fun.

It was probably just as well that somehow, thanks to Frankie and Sketchbook, Clive had found out about the jewels. Using fake clues to lure Hazel and Ned into quicksand or bear pits would have amused Clive and distracted him from jail and his looming trial. But getting them to hand over actual treasure—antique jewels, no less—that would be a challenge the con artist could not resist.

An image sprang into Hazel's mind: Clive as a puppet master, pulling the strings of an army of crows. She didn't know who the crows were; she supposed evil masterminds had a limitless supply of faceless henchmen to do their bidding. What had Ned called them: minions?

Speaking of crows, she'd better get back to the others and tell them Clive was up to his old tricks. The japer, the trickster. Of course it would be him.

Slowly, taking great care to make as little noise as possible, Hazel began to back away from the hut. From above her head, the hawk gave a warning cry. Hazel spun around and saw a crow advancing from the left. Another crow appeared on her right.

"What the heck was that?" Kenny burst out of the hut, his face white as the sheet that covered Hazel. Billy was hard on his heels.

"We've been looking for you," the taller crow said.

Hazel gulped. She opened her mouth to reply, but Kenny got there first.

"I was coming. I wasn't hiding or nothing. I was just taking a break."

"Well, your break's over."

They seemed content so far to ignore Hazel, but there was

no telling when that might change. She began edging away.

The second, sturdier crow moved closer, shaking his head. As his giant mask swung back and forth, moonlight illuminated his dead, glassy eye. The effect was so creepy, Hazel saw Billy flinch. When the crow spoke, his voice came out in a horrible croak.

"Your uncle said you'd be able to identify the Frump girl. So where is she?"

Now Hazel was rooted to the spot.

"I don't know her that well," Kenny said. "There are so many people here. We don't even know for sure she came."

"Well, what does she look like?" the second crow said.

He was losing patience, Hazel realized. And Kenny and Billy knew it too.

"She's tall, and she has red hair, and she's stupid . . . ." Kenny's voice trailed off.

The tall crow seemed to notice Hazel for the first time. "Hey, ghost—scram!"

Only too happy to oblige, Hazel picked up the folds of her sheet, the better to run without tripping.

"Wait!" Kenny Pritchard was pointing at the ground near her feet. Hazel looked down and realized he was pointing at her shoes—her high-top, special edition, "signed by Steve Nash and Candace Parker" basketball shoes. *No.*

"That's her," Kenny said.

And Hazel could hear the guilt in his voice, along with the triumph.

Hazel turned to run, but the tall crow got to her first, grabbing her arm and twisting. And then the second crow raised a wooden stick. As he swung it toward Hazel's head, she suddenly remembered the phrase she'd been searching for.

A murder of crows.

CHAPTER TWENTY-ONE

The painter bent over Hazel. She recognized him from the self-portrait he'd sketched in his diary. Except . . . he seemed younger, and so frightened. Hazel wanted to reassure him, but he was getting fainter and blurrier. He was yelling now, telling her to wake up. Then someone kicked her and everything went black—

Hazel was back at the Rose & River Inn. Moonlight drenched the limestone walls, turning them silver. This was nothing like the ruin Hazel and Ned had seen. Its gingerbread trim glistened with fresh paint; the rolling lawns were trim. A row of saplings marked the tidy path that led from the inn to The Boathouse tavern beside the riverbank. But it was the middle of the night and all was still.

No, the painter was there. He was arguing with another man, and they were struggling. The painter broke free, staggered back against the well. He opened his mouth to plead, and Hazel heard Kenny Pritchard's voice: "I don't have it. I don't know where it is. Please, it's not my fault."

Like a swimmer fighting her way from the depths to the surface, Hazel broke free of the dream, gasping for air. Her ears were ringing. Something wet and sticky had trickled down the back of her neck. Please don't let that be blood, she thought. Had she hit her head? Her brain felt fuzzy—like a radio that wasn't quite picking up a signal. Hazel started to reach a hand up to touch the stickiness. And stopped.

Her hands were tied.

It took a moment to sink in. Someone had actually bound her wrists with rope. Hazel could tell she was lying on a rough, wooden floor. How had she gotten here? How long had she been lying here? And where, exactly, was here?

Her entire body ached and her brain felt . . . unfocused. She'd felt this way once before. Last year's basketball finals. They were up by two points with seconds to go and Hazel had gone flying up to block a shot. They'd won, but at a price. As Hazel came down she fell into another player and their tangled bodies had landed badly. The other girl tore a knee ligament. Hazel wound up with a sprained ankle and a concussion.

Concussion. Yes, that's what this was. But how did she get it this time? And did it happen before or after someone tied her up?

Hazel opened her eyes. She couldn't see. For one terrible second she thought she'd been blinded, but no—something was covering her eyes. Not a blindfold. Maybe a sheet? Yes, there was a sheet over her head. Why was there a sheet over her head? Hazel frowned. Ow. Big mistake. Note to self: avoid using facial muscles. Were there any muscles she *could* use? Hazel took a deep breath and let it out slowly. Okay, ribs sore but not cracked. Tentatively, she stretched her left leg and flexed her ankle. Both okay. Ditto the left arm and hand.

The bad news was on the right. Everything on that side hurt. Hazel grunted in pain as she stretched and flexed. Nothing felt broken, but she had some messed-up ligaments and tendons.

There'd be more rehab and some killer bruises once she got out of here.

Assuming she *could* get out of here.

It would help if her brain could stay focused. But her thoughts were bouncing from one thing to another, like an arcade game. Stop, she told herself. Think. What was the last thing she could remember? Halloween. Costumes. Of course— the sheet over her head. That had been her idea. And in the end, they'd all agreed. They'd come as ghosts. Goofy, Charlie Brown–type ghosts. So she was still in her costume. The eye-holes had to be around here somewhere . . .

No. Forget about the eyeholes. Focus. It's Halloween. Or it used to be. It depended on how long Hazel had been lying here. Long enough for blood to congeal on her neck. How long did that take? Ned might know.

Ned! Where was Ned?

Hazel struggled to sit up. It wasn't easy to do, with her hands tied, but it could have been worse. On TV the police always handcuffed people with their arms behind their backs. But her hands were in front of her. Whoever had tied up Hazel had not watched enough television.

Hazel's wrists had been neatly crossed, one over the other, before they were tied. She pulled her arms closer together. Just as she'd hoped, the rope slackened. Maybe, just maybe, she could wriggle one hand right out of the loop. Hazel almost cracked a smile, but remembered in time that smiling might hurt her face. She concentrated on working her hands free. The friction from the rope burned her skin.

There. She'd done it.

Hazel pulled the sheet off her head and looked around. It was dark and cold and there was a smell like wet sweaters. What kind of place was this?

On the opposite wall, she could make out faint lines of

light—the outline of a door. Hazel groped her way to standing and a wave of nausea swept over her. No fainting, she told herself, and lurched toward the door.

It opened easily. She found herself in a large, open room with a high ceiling and a lot of old-fashioned machinery. A giant pile of wool, recently shorn, took up half the room. Well, that explained the smell.

Moonlight was flooding through a glass-paned window a few feet away.

Now Hazel knew where she was—the old mill, on the edge of the pioneer village where the islanders held their annual Halloween party. And the party was still going strong. Hundreds of people in costumes were wandering the grounds, collecting candy from the volunteers staffing the replica buildings. Hazel couldn't make out the details of any costumes, but amid the dark figures were plenty of glow-sticks and fluorescent patches bobbing along, low to the ground. It couldn't be too late yet—even the kindergarten crowd was still trick-or-treating.

As she stared out the window, Hazel realized she could hear voices coming from the floor below. Her captors. If she threw open the window and yelled, "Help!" would anyone hear her? Or would she simply draw the attention of her kidnappers instead?

Kidnapped. Until now, Hazel's mind had managed to avoid thinking the word. But it was the only thing that made sense. She didn't have time to ponder who had kidnapped her or why. There were several voices downstairs now—and they were arguing.

Hazel grasped the window sash and yanked. It rattled slightly before sliding open. She stuck her head out the window and waved, frantically. A tiny girl in a Teletubby costume who'd wandered away from her group glanced up and waved. Then she turned and skipped back into the throng. Time for the costume awards. Everyone was heading toward the Town Hall. *Away* from the mill.

Hazel pulled her head back inside. Don't panic, she told herself, just go to plan B.

But first: think up a plan B.

There was a sheer drop from this window. Impossible. What about the one on the other side of the room? Could she climb out that one and escape?

The voices downstairs were yelling now. Good, thought Hazel. That might help mask the sounds as she stumbled across the room. It's hard to tiptoe when you can't put any weight on one foot.

The view from this window was more promising. A spreading maple had grown up close to the side of the mill. She might be able to escape this way. After all, Hazel and Ned had once fled a museum by climbing out a second-storey window and down a tree.

"I'm telling you, I don't have it. I don't know where it is. Please, it's not my fault."

Hazel stopped. It was Kenny. And he sounded just as scared as he had in her dream.

"Your uncle wants that ring. If she didn't give it to you, then she must know where it is. So you're going to try one more time to wake her up, and you're going to get her to tell you where it is."

"Why me?"

"Because then I won't hurt you . . . anymore."

Think fast, Hazel told herself. Kenny was obviously in trouble, but so was she. One thing at a time: first save herself, *then* send rescue party back for local hoodlum.

Hazel had just eased the window open when she heard a *creak* on the stairs. She'd run out of time. They'd be up here in seconds, and Hazel knew from experience it would take time to climb down that tree. Time enough for the crows to be waiting for her at the foot of the giant maple.

There was no way out. Unless . . . Hazel glanced from the open window to the giant pile of wool and back. It was worth a try. Lucky she wasn't allergic to wool.

There was just enough time to toss her ghost sheet out the window and hope it would snag on a tree branch.

Footsteps sounded near the top of the stairs. At least two people. Maybe three? Hazel heard them walk across the floor and open the door to the stall. A few seconds of silence passed before one of the crows swore violently. Hazel heard the door to the stall being slammed again and again.

Now came the tricky bit. Hazel needed the crow to notice the open windows, or her plan wouldn't work. But that meant he had to come closer to her hiding place. She concentrated on breathing as quietly as possible.

"Hey." The croaky-voiced crow was crossing the room now. He was only a few feet away.

Hazel willed him to look out the window.

"Didn't you say that girl escaped from Fazza once by climbing out the window at the museum and down a tree?"

Kenny's voice was subdued. "Yeah. She did."

The crow swore again. "That's it, I'm out of here. She's probably getting the cops right now. If Clive Pritchard wants that ring so bad, he can get it himself."

Deep inside the pile of wool, Hazel heard the clattering of feet down the stairs. She didn't move. From somewhere below came the sound of a door slamming. Still, Hazel lay there, breathing silently and counting to a hundred, slowly.

When an eternity had passed, Hazel summoned all of her strength and crawled out of the pile of wool.

Kenny was sitting on the floor by the window, his back to the wall. He didn't look surprised to see her. Although Hazel wasn't sure he could see anything. His face was bruised and puffy. One eye was swollen shut.

"Hey." Kenny sniffed and wiped his nose with his sleeve. "I figured you were in there. It looked like a good place to hide."

"Oh," Hazel said. "Uh, thanks for not telling the crows, then."

She sat some distance from the boy, her back against the wall too. She wasn't sure, but she thought he was crying.

"Kenny?"

"What?"

"Are you wearing tights?"

Kenny's face contorted with anger. "I'm Robin Hood, okay? Why doesn't anybody get that?"

Hazel wanted to laugh but her side ached too much and she was still trying not to move the muscles of her face anymore than she had to.

"Seriously? As in stealing from the rich and giving to the poor? *That* Robin Hood?"

"Well, you Frumps are rich, aren't you?" Kenny wiped his nose again. "You live in a castle. You think you're so much better than us."

"I don't," Hazel began, and then she stopped. If she was being absolutely, brutally, one-hundred-percent honest, she *did* think she was better than Kenny. But it wasn't because her family had money. It was because she didn't go around bullying kids or shooting people in the back with paintball guns or helping kidnappers, or any of Kenny's other delightful hobbies.

"You need a doctor," Kenny said. "You look awful."

Hazel studied him. He didn't seem concerned, but he wasn't gloating either. He sounded almost in awe. She must look bad.

"You could use one too." Hazel shifted on the floor, trying to find a position that didn't hurt. After a few seconds she gave up. "That guy, the crow with the croaky voice, who is he?"

At first she thought Kenny wasn't going to answer. Then he shrugged.

"I don't know his name—he's not from around here. The other guys are local. You know: small-time crooks and wannabes. Some of them have worked for Uncle Clive before, a couple of 'em just owe him favours. But that guy's different, professional. I guess that's why Uncle Clive hired him; he doesn't mess around."

"He hit you, didn't he?"

Kenny turned his face away. "I *told* him I didn't know where the stupid ring was."

"Right. Why does your uncle want it so badly, anyway?"

"He thinks it's a long-lost Pritchard family heirloom. My dad says there never was a ring—it's just one of those family legends. But Uncle Clive's been looking for it forever."

Hazel nodded.

"What about the rest of the jewels?"

Kenny gave her a blank look.

"What jewels? Uncle Clive just talked about a ring." Kenny's shoulders sagged. "Uncle Clive said if I got him the ring, he'd help my dad. He'd tell the judge my dad wasn't really involved in all that smuggling and stuff, that he tricked my dad."

"Is that true?" Hazel asked. "*Did* he trick your dad?"

Kenny didn't answer.

Hazel closed her eyes. In her mind she could see the portrait hanging in Clive's shop. She could see her so clearly, that cruel-looking woman with the enormous ruby ring. She opened her eyes and stared at Kenny. "There's this painting in your uncle's shop . . ."

Kenny scowled. "There are lots of paintings in Uncle Clive's shop. And we're not allowed to sell any of them until the cops decide whether they're stolen goods."

Hazel pretended he hadn't spoken. "This painting belongs in your family, I think. It's a portrait . . . a beautiful woman in an old-fashioned dress." Hazel paused. "She kind of looks like you."

"That stupid thing?" But Hazel could tell Kenny was flattered. "It's supposed to be, I dunno, my great-great-great-great-grandmother? I forget how many greats."

"Do you know anything about her?" Hazel tried to keep her voice casual.

"Naw." Kenny sniffed. "Well, they say she died of a broken heart or something. Because her brother ran off and got killed in the war."

"What war?"

"How should I know? Vietnam, maybe."

Hazel desperately wanted to tell Kenny that the Vietnam War had been fought in the 1960s and 1970s—about a hundred years after his ancestor had posed for that portrait. And also: Canada didn't fight in the Vietnam War. But she bit her lip instead and counted to twenty. And when she was done, Hazel had a different topic for Kenny.

"So that crow, the really mean one who knocked me out," Hazel said. "I heard him tell you to try one more time to wake me up."

"So?" Kenny glared at her.

"So . . . I think I remember you trying to wake me. I thought you were someone else . . . Hey, did you *kick* me?"

She could tell Kenny was preparing to deny it. She could actually *see* his brain working on the lie. But then his eyes met hers and suddenly all his usual defiance and bluster appeared to desert him. He slumped back against the wall.

"You wouldn't wake up," he said.

Hazel wanted nothing more than to walk across the room, take Kenny by the shoulders and shake him. But she waited until she could speak calmly.

"I couldn't wake up because I was *unconscious*. You . . . That's not the same thing as napping."

Kenny was resting his head on his knees, his face hidden behind the puffy sleeves of his bright green Robin Hood costume. Hazel could feel anger churning in her stomach.

"Hey! Pay attention! You kicked me! When I was unconscious! Plus, you turned me over to those evil crows! What's wrong with you?"

"I didn't know what else to do!" Kenny raised his head to look at Hazel. She could see the tear stains on his face. Were they tears of remorse, or self-pity?

"That guy was gonna beat me up. He *did* beat me up. You think he was just kidding around? You know what he did to Charlotte!"

Something in Kenny's voice made Hazel realize that even if he hated the Frumps, he didn't hate Charlotte. She thought about all the times Charlotte had gone over to Kenny's house. She wondered if he'd been jealous about the treasure hunt. But even as Hazel started to feel the stirrings of sympathy, she hardened her heart.

"So why didn't you go to the police? And why did he attack Charlotte? She didn't have the ring. I don't even think she knows about it. Did you tell him she did?"

"No!" Kenny shook his head. "That had nothing to do with the ring or that stupid treasure hunt. He was just in the barn that night to steal a horse, and Charlotte caught him. At least that's what Uncle Clive says."

They sat in silence for a while. Hazel knew she should get up.

Her family was bound to be searching for her by now, worried out of their minds. But she was so very tired. And everything hurt. Her mouth was dry. She wondered why Kenny hadn't run away.

"Hey, Kenny? Your family's lived on this island a long time, right?"

"Sure. We go way back. The Pritchards have been here just as long as the Frumps." Kenny folded his arms across his chest, his expression a curious mixture of pride and guilt.

Hazel nodded. The pieces were sliding into place now.

"I'm kind of curious about your first name. My brother, Ned, his real name is Edwin, but nobody ever calls him that. Is Kenny short for something?" Hazel held her breath.

Kenny was staring at her out of his one good eye, like she'd lost her mind.

"Why do you care? Like I'd tell you anyway. It's a stupid name. I hate it."

"Can I guess?"

"Knock yourself out."

"Is your real name Kenton? Kenton Pritchard?"

Kenny was too dazed to deny it. He nodded, slowly, before asking, "How did you know?"

Hazel sighed. "It's a long story. You wouldn't believe me if I told you."

Kenny squinted at her and sat up a little straighter. "I got nowhere else to go right now."

So Hazel told him a story about a young painter named Kenton, who was tricked and kidnapped long ago by a strange man named Edwin Frump. A man who thought he could do magic. A japer. She described how Kenton managed to escape Edwin's clutches and make his way to a meeting with the Fenian Brotherhood, only to be killed when a fight broke out over a missing ring. A ring that then lay hidden in the castle at Land's End for more than a century, until Hazel and Ned found it, and Clive decided to steal it.

"Is any of that true?" Kenny asked, when Hazel finished speaking.

Hazel shrugged. "I guess we'll never know for sure. I can't be positive that my crazy ancestor didn't murder the other Kenton Pritchard. Or maybe he escaped and those Fenians never caught up with him and he just lived happily ever after somewhere."

"There's no such thing." Kenny's eyes were bleak. "I think the Fenians took him out. They figured he'd turned on the gang. They would have hunted him down."

"But he was never really a part of that brotherhood," Hazel said quietly. "It was just something his family got him into."

She thought at first that she had been too subtle for Kenny. But after a moment their eyes met and he gave a tiny, almost imperceptible nod.

Somewhere deep in the pocket of Hazel's jeans, something rang.

Hazel stared stupidly in the direction of the sound. Her phone! She'd completely forgotten she even owned a phone. She dug frantically in her pocket, wincing as the rough fabric rubbed the rope burns on her wrists.

"No way—you had a cell phone all this time? And you didn't call for help?" Kenny sniggered. "I guess money can't buy brains."

Hazel threw a murderous glance at him as she flipped open the phone. If she threw it hard enough at Kenny, could she blind him? At least knock out a tooth?

"I. Have. A. Concussion." She spat the words at him. "Let's see how clearly you think after getting beat up!"

But Kenny took one look at Hazel's raised fist and started to giggle. He didn't stop laughing until she'd hung up, after telling

Matt where they were, and promising not to move until he and the others arrived.

"So, what happens now?" Kenny asked.

Hazel assumed he was asking about the ring. But before she could tell him that as far as she was concerned, he could have it, Kenny spoke again.

"I mean, do you think . . . I dunno . . . Do you think, maybe, we could all just get along?"

Hazel considered him. Kenny had shot her with a paintball gun, lured her into danger with his uncle's clues, handed her over to kidnappers and kicked her while she lay helpless. On the other hand, he hadn't given her away to the evil crows a second time, when she was hiding in the wool. And he hadn't asked about the treasure, even though it was clear it rightfully belonged to his family.

"I don't know," Hazel said.

She got to her feet with difficulty and Kenny did the same. They stood facing each other. Hazel thrust her hand forward, and Kenny recoiled, as if expecting a slap. He stared at her for a moment before tentatively shaking hands.

"Maybe," Hazel said, and smiled.

The moment called for a grand exit, but all either of them could manage was a slow shuffle toward the stairs.

CHAPTER TWENTY-TWO

Charlotte's smile was rueful as she opened the pair of velvet boxes and set them on one of the library tables, for the Frumps to view.

Three days had passed since the Halloween party. Three exhausting days of police interviews, doctor's examinations, long-distance phone calls and hastily arranged flights home for the children's fathers. Charlotte still didn't have her memory back, but the hospital staff said it would likely return eventually and she should try to be patient. In the meantime, the doctors agreed Charlotte could be released from hospital if she could stay at Land's End. Uncle Seamus had agreed instantly, saying it would be a privilege for the Frumps to look after *her*, for a change.

"Compared to the lost jewels, my offerings seem pretty humble."

Wordlessly, Hazel shook her head. Each box contained a set of platinum rings; each ring held the birthstone of one of the Frump children. They were exquisitely worked, and although each could be worn on its own, the rings had been designed to fit together seamlessly. Hazel had never seen anything like them. She glanced up at her father.

"Charlotte and I were racking our brains trying to come up with a suitable ending for our treasure hunt," Colin Frump said. "And then she remembered these rings. I didn't know anything about them, of course, and when she explained their history . . ."

Hazel stared at her father. He appeared to be holding back tears.

"Well." Colin Frump coughed. "I thought they were too precious to use as prizes in a treasure hunt. But Charlotte convinced me otherwise."

"I had the rings made for your mothers—one ring for the birthstone of each child," Charlotte said. "They were so close to each other, and to their nieces and nephews—it just made sense to give them both a set representing all of you."

"I don't remember Mum wearing them—or Aunt Jane." Matt touched the rings lightly.

"Well, I only got the idea around the time your mother was expecting Oliver," Charlotte explained. "The jeweller hadn't finished them yet when . . ."

Charlotte didn't need to finish the sentence. Jane and Julia, the two sisters, were killed together in a car accident shortly after Oliver was born.

"Anyway, I'd been holding on to them for so long now, waiting for the right moment to pass them on to you kids," Charlotte continued. "And then I just thought—well, this would be fun."

Deirdre had tears in her eyes as she swooped down on Charlotte's armchair, wrapping her in an enormous hug.

"Go easy." Uncle Seamus laid a restraining hand on Deirdre's shoulder. "She's only been out of the hospital a few hours."

Charlotte laughed and made a shooing motion at Uncle Seamus.

"I'm fine. Anyway, hugs are the best medicine. And now, I want to know the whole, complete and unabridged story behind these legendary lost jewels. Whose are they, exactly, and how did they come to be lost?"

So Hazel and Ned put Kenton Pritchard's diary on the table beside the rings, along with the healing book Edwin Frump had stolen from Mercy and turned into *My Book of Spells and Magicks*. Then Hazel added Kenton Pritchard's sketches of Mercy and the old newspaper clipping about James Pritchard of Montreal that accused the Pritchards of supporting Patrick Whelan, the Fenian hanged for killing Thomas D'Arcy McGee, one of the Fathers of Confederation.

"So, Kenton Pritchard came from Montreal to paint portraits for the Frumps, and he brought his family's ruby ring with him, to hand over to the Fenians as funding for their cause?" Charlotte asked.

"Yes, but we think the other jewels in the box are what Mercy gave to Kenton, as payment for the portraits he painted," Hazel said.

"And maybe as hush money." Ned peered over the top of his glasses at the portrait of Edwin. "You know, so Kenton wouldn't tell everyone about crazy Edwin stealing his shoe-laces at night."

"We weren't sure for a long time that they were the lost jewels. We thought at first they might be the ones you and Dad hid, because all our birthstones are there," Hazel said.

Charlotte grinned. "Yes, trust you Frumps to have only precious gems for your birthstones!"

Matt studied the portrait of Mercy Frump. "I wonder if she ever learned the truth about what happened to the painter."

Ned produced the old copies of the *Frontenac Gazette*, pointing the adults to the article about the Rose & River Inn being used as a Fenian hangout, and to the story about the well being moved, in a search for better water. And Hazel showed them the local history written by the clergyman's wife.

"So we don't know for sure, but we think either Kenton Pritchard escaped, or Edwin let him go, but without the ring and the other jewels." Hazel paused, remembering the way her mind, in dreams, had begun fitting the pieces of the puzzle together. "If that deathbed confession was true, it's possible the Fenians killed Kenton Pritchard when he showed up without the ring, and then they dumped the body down the well. No one ever found it because they were digging a new well anyway."

"And Mercy sent Edwin off to England to some kind of nuthouse, and told everyone he was studying taxidermy." Mark shook his head. "I found some wacky stuff on the Internet about Victorian taxidermists—most of them were more like naturalists, you know, using their work as research on wildlife. But some of them liked to pose the animals as if they were people—having parties, preparing meals. Freaky."

"I don't even want to think about why it was Edwin's hobby." Matt's expression was bleak. "Poor Mercy, having to deal with a brother like that."

"Yeah—not like you, bro." Mark grinned. "They don't come any finer than me and young Oliver here—well, and Ned's like an honorary brother."

"Speaking of sisters and brothers, I found out something about that portrait in Clive Pritchard's shop." Hazel looked at Ned. "Kenny said the woman is his ancestor—some kind of great-great-great-great-grandmother. I think she was Kenton's sister. Kenny said she died of a broken heart after her brother ran off to join a war. There wasn't exactly a real war going on back then, but it sort of fits."

Ned nodded. "The Pritchard family could have figured Kenton just joined the Fenians and never came back."

"But I'll bet the Pritchards still had their doubts about the Frumps." Matt frowned. "Considering Edwin and Mercy had to be the last people to see Kenton alive. And they probably only needed to spend five minutes with Edwin to realize he was nuts."

"The Frumps and the Pritchards." Colin Frump looked thoughtful. "It reminds me of the Montagues and the Capulets."

"Or the Black Donnellys and the Farrells," Mark offered. "No, wait—it's the Jets and the Sharks."

"But which are we?" asked Deirdre.

"Exactly!" the twins replied together.

"We have no idea who you're talking about," Ned said sternly. "And we don't want to know. I think we should leave the nineteenth century in the past for now. I vote we go shoot some hoops."

"Great idea." Mark hopped out of his chair. "Everyone but Hazel and Charlotte—they're benched."

"Benched?" Hazel raised her eyebrows.

"Those eyebrows are probably the only body parts you can move without wincing," Colin Frump said dryly.

"Yeah, Charlotte's too weak to play, and you're too banged up." Mark patted Hazel on the head. "You've got bruised ribs, cuts, a sprained ankle, and who knows what else. You need to take it easy. You can just watch."

Ned snorted. "Watch? You really don't know my sister at all, do you?"

But in the end Hazel was content to let the others play. Huddling with Charlotte on the bench, sipping a mug of steaming hot chocolate, Hazel didn't feel left out. Her body needed to mend, and she had nothing to prove. She could just sit here and enjoy the sight of tiny Ned crossing over on tall, gangly Mark. Her dad was right—even laughing hurt. But it was worth it. There was no way she'd be in shape to play when school started up again, but Hazel realized she didn't care anymore about that starting point guard spot.

Let Georgia have a shot, Hazel thought from the sidelines. I'll be back.

EPILOGUE

Hazel sat in the centre of her tower bedroom, packing for the return to school. Nearly one month had passed since the freak storm had wreaked its damage, but it felt much longer. The major repairs had been done and the schools were reopening; Hazel's battered body had begun to mend. She'd miss Land's End and her family, but she was ready to go back.

Hazel couldn't wait to hear what her teammates would say when they traded stories of how they'd spent the break.

"I'm glad Uncle Seamus and Dad agreed to turn the treasure over to Kenny's mother," Ned said.

"Just the ring," Hazel reminded him. "Dad's buying Mercy's jewels back from her, to keep them in the family, and the money's going into a trust fund for Kenny."

"He doesn't need a trust fund," Ned said. "He needs a get-out-of-jail-free card."

Hazel said nothing. She still hadn't made up her mind about Kenny. Hazel had told the police the truth about how he'd helped the cruel crow kidnap her. But she'd done her best to be fair, making sure the police also knew that Kenny had been threatened and hurt and that he'd stayed silent in the mill when he could have exposed her. Kenny had already agreed to testify against Clive on the kidnapping charges and Uncle Seamus said that would help Kenny's case.

But no one knew exactly what lay in store for him.

The Frumps had all agreed it was time to at least try to end the families' feud, and Hazel liked the idea of peace. She just wasn't sure how easy that would be, with several members of the Pritchard family in jail.

"Hey, Hazel?" Ned's voice was filled with awe. "There's some-one at your window."

Hazel glanced up. A hawk was perched on the sill, his golden eye surveying her, unblinking. They stared at each other for a moment, and then the bird soared into the sky, swooping low over the apple orchard, before flying out across the lake. Hazel watched him go, wondering if somehow, by solving the mys-tery—but no, his wing was still crooked.

"So that was a hawk, right? Like in your dream? Wild. Hey, what's this?"

Ned was sitting on the floor beside her bed. Now he reached behind him and pulled a crumpled windbreaker from beneath Hazel's bed. "Oh man, you complain about me being messy—isn't this the jacket you've been looking for ever since you got here?"

He tossed the wadded ball of nylon toward her. Something clattered to the floor. Hazel picked it up. It was a key.

"Where'd you get that?" Ned asked.

Hazel turned the key over in her hands. She started to say that she didn't know, but suddenly an image flashed into her mind: a terrible storm lashing the forest at Land's End, and a hawk guiding her to safety. And Hazel could see herself reaching into a hollow tree and pulling out something small and cold and made of metal.

"What's it for?" Ned was staring at her.

"I don't know." Hazel smiled. "But I can't wait to find out."

ACKNOWLEDGEMENTS

The sophomore challenge is everything it's cracked up to be. For their insight, advice, reassurance and keen editorial eyes (while reading horrid, early drafts), I am greatly indebted to Carolyn Kennedy and Carol Jupiter. They do not realize the importance of their talent and friendship.

Without my patient and gifted editor, Lynne Missen, I could not have turned those early drafts into this book. Thanks are also due to Patricia O'Campo, Noelle Zitzer and Liza Morrison, whose enthusiasm sustains so many.

During the ups and downs I was buoyed again by Vicky Gall; Joe, Emily and Andrew Pepper; Maxine Hersch; Stan Dinoff; Heather Mallick; Stephen Petherbridge; Nancy Eisenhauer; Doug Kelly; Susan Opler; Barbara McKegney; Bronwynne, Declan and Gareth Dawes; Lina Loparco; Mike Rogers; and the runners: Julie Cohen, Paige Cowan, Claire Cram, Gillian Cummings, Janet Deacon, Sue Doyle, Ruth Durgy, Chris Filipiuk, Heather Gardiner, Susan Gordon, Julia Holland, Katharine Lake-Berz, Michelle Martin, Maryse Roy, Carrie Scace and Carol Wildi. And I will always be grateful to William Monahan, whose cheerful intelligence gave us something to look forward to each week.

ACKNOWLEDGEMENTS

Buzz Lanthier-Rogers and Nicky Lanthier-Rogers listened to early chapters and their advice was always excellent. James Lanthier-Rogers encouraged me to keep going, and his faith was inspiring. And when I needed to escape, Sadie Frame and Sheelagh Frame let me write for days on end in their library. I am forever in their debt.

But without Stephen Rogers, this book would not exist. I hope he enjoys *The Legend of the Lost Jewels*.